THE KING'S SPINSTER BRIDE

RUBY DIXON

RUBY DIXON

THE KING'S SPINSTER BRIDE

Sixteen years ago, Princess Halla of Yshrem saved the life of an eight-year-old barbarian boy and watched her kingdom fall to ruin, all on the same day. Now, she is a forgotten spinster in a quiet temple, living her days out in solitude. The last of her line, she exists in the hope that she has been forgotten, for to be remembered by the enemy is to be certain death.

One person has not forgotten her. Mathior, now twenty-four, is the fierce warrior king of the Cyclopae. Yshrem is in turmoil and his advisors have a suggestion – kill the last remaining member of the royal line, and there will be no rivals for the throne.

Mathior has a different idea. He's loved Halla for sixteen long years, and it's time he claimed her as his wife. But a barbarian's wedding customs are unlike any other...

1

Sixteen Years Ago

HALLA

"*I* thought cyclops were supposed to have one eye, not two," titters one of my attendants. "Are we quite sure that he's Alistair's son?" The other women in the room giggle behind their sewing.

I ignore them, gently pushing my needle through my embroidery. The boy in question stands by the castle window, looking out over the city. Yshrem is unnaturally quiet this time of day. It's because the walls are manned against the army waiting outside, ready to put us under siege unless my father the king surrenders.

My father won't surrender, though. He's too proud. Yshrem and all its lands belong to him. He is a good ruler, I think. Fair and wise. Maybe a bit intractable when crossed, but I adore him and hope to rule like him someday. King Gallin the wise. King Gallin the just. King Gallin who stands at the gates of the city, confronting Alistair and his Cyclopae warriors. I cannot help but worry, and my stitches are calm but uneven. My father is not a warrior. His hair is snowy white, and while he still stands straight, I know his knees pain him on rainy days. He surrounds himself with scholars, not generals.

Alistair's people are...not anything like us.

I think of the legends I have been told. The Cyclopae are utterly fierce and fearless. They have but one eye, stand seven feet tall and drink the blood of wolves when they are born. Their mothers do not suckle them but abandon them to the wild, and when they grow of age, they join Alistair's fierce band. They ride upon the backs of beasts and eat the flesh of their enemies. They are not civilized, not in the slightest.

I pretend to keep my eyes on my stitching and let my gaze slide over to the boy that stares out the window, his hands on his little belt. Mathior has been with us a month now, a prisoner of war. A guarantee against Alistair's wrath, my father said. It has not seemed to work, because Alistair has shown up at Yshrem with an army, and I worry things will not end peaceably. Mathior does not look much like the legends, I have to admit to myself. He is just a boy of eight, and while he is tall and browned from the sun, he does not look as if he eats the flesh of his enemies. He has two eyes, and they are a soft brown that is almost as dark as his long, braided hair. Although he has been with us for a month, he chooses to wear the clothing of his people, preferring his fur vest and soft suede leggings to the decorated fabrics of my father's court. His hands rest at his waist, as if he is hoping for a dagger to appear there.

And he watches the walls of the city intently.

The handmaids giggle again. "If he's not a cyclops, then what is he?" one of them asks.

"A bastard?" suggests another.

I push my needle through my banner. "Enough. Mathior is a guest, and an honored one."

"He is a savage, my princess—"

I give her a sharp look and she goes quiet. Of course she falls silent. She would not dare displease Crown Princess Halla of Yshrem, sole heir to the throne. It doesn't matter that I'm barely sixteen. I've never been allowed to be a child. I am the heir first, a marriageable bride second, and a daughter last. For the last few months, ever since my birthday approached, the kingdom has been besieged with suitors from distant, far-flung kingdoms who wish to marry me and "help" rule Yshrem. I know my marriage must be one of convenience and not love, so I have kept all at arm's length and showed interest in none...even if my girlish heart secretly yearns for one or two of the more handsome, dashing lordlings.

Marriage will be a certain part of my future. To choose otherwise would make the kingdom unstable, because right now I am the only heir. I have always known that I will be married off for a strong alliance, so I have never allowed myself to dream of love except in secret.

Not that love matters. Or marriage. On this day, marriage is the furthest thing from my mind. It is the fate of the kingdom itself I worry over. The walls of the castle shake, and screams echo up from the courtyard, and my next stitch is shaky. I force myself to remain focused even as a few of my ladies nervously get to their feet, heading for the window. They stare down at the siege below us, and when one of the women pales and returns to her seat next to me, I know it is not going well.

Alistair has come for his son. The Cyclopae, savage barbarians all of them, have laid siege to the graceful, cultured kingdom of

Yshrem. I tell myself they are the barbarians, not us. I tell myself that we are far ahead of them in advancements and armor and courtly tactics on the battlefield. We should win handily.

But the Yshremi have lost every battle against the cyclops. And now they are on our doorstep, and I am filled with fear.

"Princess," Lady Tamira retakes her chair next to mine, and her face is white with fear. "They have broken through the gates. Shall we go into hiding?"

I swallow hard and force myself to do another calm stitch. "No. My father's troops will handle it." I can't retreat. To do so would show that I have no faith in my father to defeat his enemies. If word of that got out, we would be attacked from all sides even if we were to repel the cyclops invaders. It does not matter. Fight one enemy or fight all of them.

I notice Mathior comes to my side. For such a small boy, he's remarkably observant and acts far older than he is. He watches me with dark eyes as I do my best to continue my embroidery even though my hands are shaking. After a moment, he puts a hand on my shoulder. "It's all right, Halla. My father's going to win this day, but I will tell him of your bravery."

I look at him in surprise, at his tanned face and dark eyes, the long, wild hair decorated with feathers and fur. Even though he has been with my people for nearly a month, he refuses to dress like a courtier and prefers to seem a barbarian.

"How dare you!" Lady Tamira exclaims, rushing forward to snatch young Mathior's hand from my shoulder. "First of all, she is Princess Halla to you. And you are not allowed to touch her!" She sniffs indignantly at the thought.

"But I am a prince," Mathior says, his expression growing childishly stubborn. "Why can't I talk to her as if she's my equal?"

"Because you are a barbarian," Tamira hisses. She holds her skirts out as if blocking him from my view, and my lips twitch with amusement when Mathior simply crosses his eyes at her. "Your people are strange and crude and are not fit to lick the princess's shoes."

"Lady Tamira," I begin again, ready to correct her.

Before I can, Mathior speaks up. "It is your people who are the strange ones," Mathior says. "Mine are warriors." He holds himself up proudly to his full eight-year-old height. "And by the end of this day, you will be bowing to me."

My lady-in-waiting squawks indignantly, but before I can step in, the door to my private chambers flies open. The royal guard rushes in, accompanied by Lord Balun, one of my father's close friends and advisors. I jump to my feet, forgetting to be ladylike and calm. Balun's clothes are streaked with blood and his eyes are wild. He scans the room and at the sight of Mathior, points a dagger. "There he is, men. Grab the little heathen."

I suspected this might happen, and that is why the barbarian prisoner is in my apartments this day, with my ladies. I calmly step in front of Mathior, as if this is nothing out of the ordinary, and give Lord Balun a cool look. "What are you doing? Who gave you permission to enter my chambers?"

"Forgiveness, Princess," he tells me breathlessly even as I shift and hide the cyclops boy behind my skirts. His hands clutch at them and I can feel his small form tremble behind me, for all that he's never shown fear before. It reminds me that he is still very much a young child, nine years younger than me. It might as well be a lifetime. Balun straightens, his face pale. "We are lost, Princess. The Cyclops king Alistair has broken through our defenses and slaughtered your father and his guard. They are overtaking the castle." His voice breaks on a sob. "They cut him down like he was nothing! Like he was filth!" His nostrils flare and an inhuman look crosses his face. "Give me the boy. We can avenge your father and make Alistair pay, but we must be quick."

I stand there in shock. His words hit me like crossbow bolts. Father dead. The castle lost. The cyclops warriors have won. Our kingdom will be ground beneath the heel of a barbarian usurper.

I want to be strong and decisive. To be the queen they need. "My father is dead?" I whisper brokenly.

I feel Mathior's small hand clasp mine. He gives me a squeeze, as if comforting me.

Balun nods, grief and rage written on his features. Behind him, the royal guard are restless but also tormented by their failure. They do not lie to me. They have tears in their eyes, all of these men. Their king is dead and they have failed him.

"Give me the boy," Balun says again. "We can have vengeance for your father. We will cut his throat and throw his body from the battlements to show Alistair that we are unbroken—"

"No."

Lord Balun looks astonished at my refusal. His face darkens and he takes a menacing step forward, moving far too close to me for comfort. My ladies, who are not trained to be more than companions, retreat. I stand my ground and hold Mathior behind me. "Give me the boy," he says again. "This is a man's matter, not a woman's. You do not know of war. You did not see your father's death under their spears—"

"My father is dead," I say crisply, and even though I am screaming inside, I sound cool and efficient. "And your response is to kill a small boy who should not have been stolen in the first place? We are a kingdom of light and learning. That is a cowardly move and we are better than that."

I sound strong, even if my knees are weak.

"Kill him or be put to the sword yourself, Princess. Do you think the cyclops will have mercy on you? The daughter of their enemy? They will cut you down," he snarls in my face, so close that I can feel his spittle fleck my skin.

Mathior tries to move forward, but I push him behind my full skirts and press closer to my carved chair so he cannot do something as foolish as trying to save me.

"Do not stand in my way—"

"If my father is dead, I am now the queen. You are my royal guard." I give Balun and his men an imperious look. "Do you go against my wishes? Mathior is an honored guest. He will remain so. I will not let you touch him so long as I live."

"Then you will only live for an hour," snarls Balun. He turns to the royal guard.

They look at him, then at me, and drop to a knee, bowing their heads in my direction. Loyal, brave men. I stand a little bit straighter at their allegiance. I know I am right. It is not our way to kill prisoners, especially a small boy who has done nothing wrong save be born to the enemy king.

Balun turns his back to me and storms out of the room.

I blink rapidly. Everything is happening so fast. I take a deep, steeling breath as the sounds of battle below grow louder. Mathior's small hand squeezes mine, lending me his strength, and I remember who I am. Yshrem is supposed to be a good place, a cultured kingdom of learning and beauty. We are not murderers. Even if we are conquered.

Even if I am queen for ten minutes, I will be the right kind of queen.

I turn around and look at the seats scattered about my chamber. "Cosira, bring your chair next to mine," I say, indicating the next largest carved seat. "Mathior will sit at my side as the guest he is." My ladies bustle into activity and I sit back down on my chair— now my throne—and ignore the pulse hammering in my throat. I swallow hard and lift my head to address the guard waiting for my orders. "If the castle is lost and my father dead, then I would have no more blood shed on this day. Go and give the orders to lay down their weapons. Not all of my father's men need to die for Yshremi pride." I smooth my skirts and gaze upon them as a queen. "We will wait here to greet Alistair the Conqueror."

I pray that when Alistair puts his sword to my throat to kill me— as he surely will—I will be as composed as I am in this moment.

Mathior puts his hand over mine, his skin dark against my milk-pale, his hand childish against my larger one. "I won't forget, Halla."

I give his hand a squeeze and then wait to meet my end.

2

Sixteen Years Later

MATHIOR

$\mathcal{I}$ stare at my father's funeral pyre, the flames of it growing higher by the moment. Songs rise into the night, my people singing up to the stars of my father's deeds. Of the many bloody battles he fought and won. Of how he made the cyclops a kingdom to be feared. Of his conquest of Yshrem with its weakling king and neighboring Adassia, whose citizens threw down their arms the moment they heard the barbarian king had turned his eye their way. On and on, I hear songs of Alistair's many feats—some not entirely true, but all glorious and praising of his name.

This is a time for fine words in his memory. This is a time to drink and praise him. In the morning, there will be kingdoms to govern and my people to lead, but tonight is for him. At least, that is how it should be. Already his advisors look to me with questions in their eyes.

And I am the one that must give them answers.

I rub at the scar over my eye, the symbol of my strength as a warrior. The day I sacrificed my eye to the god Aron of the Cleaver to prove that I did not need two eyes to be a brutal fighter. That a fierce Cyclopae warrior only needs partial sight to ruthlessly slaughter his enemies. It is a tradition as old as time amongst my people, and I submitted willingly. That was the day I became a man, but sometimes the scar itches, even though the eye there has been long gone these ten years.

I lower my eyepatch once more and cross my arms, deliberately staring into my father's funeral pyre. I keep my gaze focused, daring the Yshremi ambassador who skulks at the edges of the celebration to come and demand answers.

I will give him answers at the tip of my spear if he does.

But the man has some brains. He gives me worried looks but does not disturb me as I pay tribute to my father. I celebrate with the others, raising my voice in song and lifting drinking horn after drinking horn in his name. I do not drink from all of them, but the revelers who celebrate my father's life—warriors and widows alike—do not notice. All they know is that they must shout their joy of my father's deeds to the heavens so the gods will hear them. Tomorrow will be a time for mourning, but not tonight.

The hours wear on, voices grow hoarse, and the fires grow dim. When the last of the flames have gone out and my father's funeral celebration is complete, I am weary but pleased. My father has been sent to the gods with great honor.

Tired, I toss my furred cloak over my shoulders and leave behind the funereal fires, toward the largest tent in the encampment. Now it is my tent.

"A word, King Mathior," I hear a voice whine from behind me.

I grit my teeth. I had hoped to wait until tomorrow to answer this. I know what he will ask. I know my answer. I have always known my answer. But I do not have the time or the patience to explain it to him or anyone else. Of course, a king should not have to explain...but warriors and diplomats are very different kinds of people. Diplomats insist on words for everything, even when I would rather shove a spear down their throats.

My father would laugh at my sourness. He would tease me and tell me that even the word-sparring is still a battle that a king must fight, and it must be approached as seriously as any battle-field combat. My throat aches and I feel a sad sense of longing that he is not here, that I must take the throne upon his death. I would give a thousand good horses if he could rule forever. I have always wanted to be king, of course, but never at his expense.

I turn and glare at the robed man who follows behind me, scrolls tucked under his arm. "The embers of my father's funeral pyre yet burn," I caution the ambassador. "Do you wish me to light a new fire for your funeral?"

"I know this is the wrong moment to approach," the man continues, cringing. I have reluctant admiration for him, because he speaks even though he knows my displeasure. "King Mathior, one of your kingdoms is in the greatest of unrest—"

"Yshrem. I know of it."

I know my father ignored it in the last few years for lands with better hunting and more glory. Yshrem is a placid place, of people who till fields instead of hunt game. Of people who cover themselves in layers upon layers of scratchy fabrics instead of soft furs, and love words instead of deeds. Of people who hide behind stone walls before their barbarian overlords. They were easy to conquer sixteen years ago, my father bragged.

I think of their lovely princess, she with the soft hands and the gentle eyes. Dark hair, a full mouth, and a steel-forged spirit. Halla. I have not forgotten her.

"Then you know that your father neglected his lands in the last few seasons," the ambassador says bluntly. "Yshrem's people feel abandoned. They are taxed and their wealth sent to the cyclops overlords but receive nothing but more burdens in return. There is not enough food, because it has all been sold to Adassia to pay taxes. There are riots in the capital, thieves and banditry upon every road and poachers in every forest. Your border overlords placed by your father grow careless and drunk with their power because he put no boundaries on them, and the people resent the fact that they steal everything from sheep to firstborn daughters and claim that it is their right as cyclopean emissaries."

"Do they now?" I drawl, thinking vaguely of the men at the keeps that have been established as border lords. Not cyclops warriors. They have two eyes and little battle in their heart for all that they bend the knee for my people. They were chosen to act as ruling lords who remained in one place, as most Cyclopae tribes are nomadic. I vaguely remember a few of Yshrem's lordlings who eagerly bowed their heads and were put in positions of power so long as they would raise no army against my father.

I knew Yshrem had been ignored. As my father's mind grew distant and the disease took more of his health, he turned to the hunt and the old ways. It is not a bad thing to live in such a manner...but a conqueror must be aware of all his kingdoms or they will turn against him.

It sounds as if the lordlings have already begun so.

The man continues on, an urgent look on his thin face. "You are in danger of losing control of the kingdom, your majesty—"

"I am not anyone's majesty," I tell him. Such titles are another Yshremi custom I dislike intensely. I do not mind "king" because it is a word that translates no matter the tongue, but speaking of my "majesty" is foolishness. "Call me First Warrior if you prefer."

"First Warrior," the man continues smoothly, trotting behind me as I push back the flap and stride into my private tent. "Of course. But you must heed my words. If you wish to stop an uprising of the people, you must do something. As long as there is a princess of the old blood, there will never be rest. Even now, insurgents call her name in the streets and demand that Queen Halla be restored to her throne."

Queen Halla.

Queen for an hour, perhaps. I smile at the thought of her. My memories are clouded by years that have passed, but I remember her braided hair, gleaming like chestnuts and her skin as pale as a winter sky. The pretty curve of her mouth. I remember how elegant she was, and how kind. How soft her hands, and how pink her lips.

She ruined me for all other women with a glimpse, and I was but a boy of eight.

"So the people make unreasonable demands. What would you have me do about that?" I ask absently, shrugging off my cloak as I near my pallet of furs. My mind is still full of Halla herself, her stiff posture and full skirts. I have dreamed of her for years, imagining laying her down in the furs of my bed and pushing those skirts up to explore what lies underneath.

One does not think such things about a princess, but that has never stopped me.

"I have a simple solution," the ambassador says.

Things are never simple, but now I am intrigued. I push thoughts of the lovely princess away. "I am listening."

"Send an assassin," the man tells me bluntly. "Take care of the problem. If she is not alive, she cannot take the throne. She has no issue. The royal line of Yshrem dies with her. It is not a pleasant solution, but a neat one. A necessary one." His voice is full of distaste, and it is clear to me that he doesn't like what he suggests, but he can see no other way out.

Such is the life of a diplomat—offering terrible solutions to their king and hoping someone else will take the blame. I am not surprised that he has offered it. It is custom among many peoples to have rivals murdered and removed quietly. It is not the cyclopean way, for we prefer to meet on the battlefield and spill blood in the name of Aron of the Cleaver.

I am not surprised that he has suggested it...but I am surprised at the violent urge that rises inside me. Not to murder Halla—but to murder anyone that suggests such a thing.

She is mine.

She has always been mine.

She will always be mine.

I keep my expression calm and unbuckle my sword belt. It has been a long day and tomorrow will be busy as well. "No one will touch Princess Halla. I have another idea," I tell him. It is an idea I have nurtured for many years in secret, one that I did not dream of pursuing while my father was alive. Now that he is gone and Yshrem is in chaos, the thought has been on my mind.

Daily. Hourly.

And who is here to tell me no? I am now First Warrior. My word is law. I can do as I like to rule my kingdoms.

"Your...er, First Warrior, I must beg you to heed me. Yshrem is a problem," the man continues. "We must do something, and we must do it soon. A show of authority is needed, and quickly—"

"It is handled." I remove my bracers, tugging at the leather ties.

"How?"

And I tell him.

When I am done explaining my beautifully simple plan, he stares at me in surprise. "You would do such a thing for your kingdom? For Yshrem and the Cyclops tribes both?"

I cannot help but smile. He thinks I do this for Yshrem? Amusing. I care nothing for Yshrem.

I do this for me, because I am now First Warrior. I am king.

And I get everything I want.

3

HALLA

*T*he early morning light is the best time to read by. I sit in the courtyard of the temple, a volume of Riekki's Prayers in my hands. At least, the binding is of Riekki's Prayers, but the interior is love poems. Reading for pleasure—especially such daring reading—is forbidden in the temple of the goddess of Peace. But when peddlers come to the temple, I am able to sneak a purchase of a book or two upon occasion.

It's the only treat I allow myself. My cell is the same gray, windowless cell of Riekki's peacekeepers. My braids are done in the manner of the temple guardians. My gown is the shapeless gray of her priesthood. I follow the rigid guidelines of the clergy. I eat no meat and live on bread and vegetables from the gardens. I do my allotted chores. I sing with the other priestesses every night in the Hour of Prayers to honor the goddess.

Truly, no one would remember I was a queen for an afternoon so many years ago, or that I once wore sumptuous robes and spent my days planning how I would rule my kingdom.

No one would imagine that I was to marry a king. Now I am an old spinster, forgotten by all. I will die loveless and alone, surrounded by gray walls and gray clothes and gray lives.

Surely a forbidden book is not such a terrible thing, then.

I turn the page in my poetry and notice there is a drawing in this book. A scandalous one. Quickly, I lift my head and glance around, but the courtyard is silent of all but a few birds. The greens of the herb gardens perfume the air, but it is too early for Peacebringer Asita to be awake to weed them.

I'm alone. Biting my lip, I furtively open the book once more and study the drawing.

It's a man with a long braid, kneeling under a woman's skirts and his face is pressed between her thighs. His tongue is obscenely poked out and it looks as if he's licking her most secret parts. What madness is this? I turn the book sideways, wondering if perhaps I am looking at it wrong. When I was princess of Yshrem, I had many ladies who prepared me with stories of what would be expected when I became a bride. Of how I would submit to my husband's carnal requests. Of the duties that would be required as a royal bride.

I'd never been told about licking.

Surely that would be something someone would mention.

"Your majesty?"

I slam the book shut, my cheeks crimson. "I'm just praying."

"Of course. I am sorry to interrupt." The priestess bows at me, her iron-gray braids dangling over her shoulders as she leans forward. "You have visitors."

I feel a little flustered at being caught and get to my feet, clutching the book to my breast. "You know the terms of my existence here. I cannot receive anyone." If I do, if I so much as turn an eye to the throne, I'll be dead. I know this, and I'm not ready to die yet, so I live a quiet life as best I can and read love poetry in private. I can live the life of a forgotten spinster, no more. The priestesses here know this, but sometimes someone forgets. I, however, must never forget. "I cannot see whoever it is. Princess Halla must not exist. Please send them on their way."

The priestess hesitates. "I...I cannot, your majesty." She wrings her hands, and a look of distress crosses her placid face.

A cold prickle moves over the back of my neck.

I know what this is. I know why she cannot send my visitors away.

This is the day I have been dreading for sixteen years. I knew it was bound to come. A person of royal blood is never truly forgotten. I knew that once I entered this temple, that I would never leave. That someday, someone would remember that the princess of Yshrem was alive and would make plans to kill her. I have heard of the riots in the capital and prayed that my name would not come up. I knew that people were starving and angry over the rules that the Cyclopae overlords have placed upon them, but I have forced such things from my mind. To get involved is to ask to get knifed in a shadowy corner.

When I first came to Riekki's temple, despite the reassurances that I was safe, I worried over such things. I never ate unless another tasted it first. I went nowhere alone. I anticipated assassins around every corner. But as one year turned into five and five into more, I felt safe. Worry faded, just like my youth and beauty. I've felt safe.

Now those fears come rushing back to me, and I want to vomit.

I force myself to remain still, to be outwardly calm. I knew this day would come. I could not be left here forever. And yet now that my death has arrived...I am not ready for it. I must meet it with dignity and grace as any royal of the throne of Yshrem...but I am not ready.

I still want to live, even if my existence is that of quiet and solitude amongst Riekki's worshipers.

But choices were taken from me long ago. I hold the book in tight fingers and lift my chin. "Send them in and please leave. Please tell everyone to stay away until my visitors depart." If assassins have come to dispatch me to the realm of the gods, I do not want them to harm any of the priestesses here. Riekki's people have been good to me. I will not have them taken down in my name.

She nods and exits quickly, her steps brisk. She does not look me in the eye, and I know I am correct. This is the hour I have dreaded.

I ponder sitting down on the bench again to hide the tremble in my body and decide to stand tall and proud instead. I wonder what the face of King Alistair's assassin will look like. Will he be kind? Will the method he chooses of dispatching me be swift and painless? If I have to choose, I pray it is not poison, or torture. I do not think I am strong enough to withstand a long, drawn-out death.

Then again, no one has asked me.

The courtyard is utterly silent, the only sound that of the birds chirping nearby. I hear boots before I hear the rustle of clothing of those that approach, the creak of leather and swish of heavy cloaks, and the jangle of metal buckles. My stomach lurches, but I remain utterly still, my face calm.

It would be very undignified to puke in front of my assassins.

Four men enter, and a cold chill moves over me. Though I try to memorize all their faces, I am drawn to one man in particular. He stands in the lead, wearing a cloak of pure white fur, his long black hair shaven on one side of his head and flowing down the other. An eyepatch covers half of his face and he's tanned and clean-shaven. Other than the cloak, he wears no clothing except for crude leather leggings and boots with metal buckles. Swords are at his belt and behind him, each of his one-eyed men carry a pair of spears crossed over their backs.

Cyclops warriors.

"Greetings," I call out in as cool a voice as I can manage. "To what do I owe this honor?"

To my surprise, the tall, handsome man in the lead breaks into a grin as he strides forward. Flustered, I force myself to remain still as he approaches. He's gorgeous. That smile dazzles me and makes my knees weak. I shouldn't be affected like this at the sight of a handsome man. He's come to kill me. I should be focused on the knives at his waist and not the beauty of his smile.

Clearly being a spinster has addled my brains.

I force myself to study the group, to focus on something other than the bare pectorals before me. I focus instead on the white fur cloak. I read somewhere that only those who have proven themselves can wear white fur—and the others look to him with deference. He is their leader, then.

"Princess Halla. I see the years have been kind to you," the handsome man says as he approaches me. He does not reach for his knife. Yet.

Have the years been kind, then? There are no mirrors here, for Riekki's people eschew vanity as one of the great sins. This man speaks as if we are familiar, though, and I do not recognize him. I study his face, the handsome, high cheekbones, the bronzed skin, the muscles that bulge underneath his cloak. I can feel myself blushing again. My life here has been one of utterly sheltered obeisance. I do not know any cyclops—any man for that matter—and I am pretty sure I would remember one this handsome.

He is young, too. Younger than me, and I have been here in this place for over sixteen years. "You have me at a disadvantage, sir. I do not know you."

His grin grows wider, and it is white as snow in his rugged face. "No, I expect you do not. I am a little different than when I was a boy." He raises a hand into the air, gesturing at his head. "I've grown a bit taller."

Boy? Taller? A flash of memory floods through me. I stare up at him, trying to see the small, quiet child in this handsome, authoritative man. "Mathior?"

"So you do remember."

My lips part, but no honorable greeting comes from my throat. This man does not look like the small boy I remember. Mathior was a tiny boy with big, dark eyes, wild hair, and a somber appearance. The man before me smiles with pleasure as he gazes at me, and while his eye is still dark, one is gone. And he is tall now, so very tall that he towers over me. "I...oh. Yes, I remember you. You look well, Prince Mathior."

"First Warrior Mathior," he corrects. "Or King Mathior, if you prefer. My father is dead and all of King Alistair's lands have fallen under my control. I now rule in his place. And that includes Yshrem and Adassia."

I feel dizzy. King Alistair is dead. That means Mathior has come to murder me to secure his claim on the throne. "I see." I didn't know that my assassin would come bearing a friendly face. I study him for a long moment, because he seems to be waiting for something. My tears? My anger? Defiance?

I have known this day would come for years, though. So I hold my book tightly to my chest and try not to think that my corpse will be found with a tome full of dirty pictures. That cannot be helped. "Will you make it swift? In the name of our friendship these many years past?"

He tilts his head, the long hair on one side of his head spilling over his shoulder. "Make what swift?"

"My death."

Mathior—if it is him—lets his mouth crook up in a smile, a somber one that tells me that yes, this is indeed the boy I once knew. "I am not here to kill you, Halla."

"Are you not?"

"Never."

The firmness of that response throws me off. I purse my lips, frustrated and doing my best not to tremble visibly. "Then I do not understand the purpose of your visit."

The look in his dark eye is strangely direct. "Do you not?" When I shake my head, he reaches out and grabs one of my thick braids, running his hand down it. It is a curiously intimate touch, one that makes my belly pool with heat and flutters of nervousness. I realize how close he's standing. "Do you recall that when my father took Yshrem, his men stormed your chambers and demanded to throw my body over the walls to anger my father?"

I remember. I remember my helpless anger at the thought of doing something to such a small, helpless boy. Of taking the frustrations of war out on a child. But mostly, I remember Mathior's small hand clasping mine as I hid him behind my skirts. The moment is etched in my mind. "I do."

"And do you remember what I told you when you said you would surrender to my father?"

I shake my head. The afternoon that day was a blur. I vaguely remember my grief at my father's death, the sight of his head on a pike as the barbarians swept through the streets and into the castle. I remember my terror as I tried to sit on my throne without collapsing. I remember wearing the crown jewels of Yshrem for a very short hour only to be brought, on my knees, to Alistair the barbarian and his men on the front lines. I remember how they called and called for my death. They wanted to see me beheaded.

And yet I wasn't. I was taken directly to Riekki's temple and left here to dwell in peace. Alistair, who never showed mercy or kindness to his foes, let his rival's heir go free. It didn't make sense. "I don't recall, I'm afraid."

"I told you I would keep you safe. That I would protect you because you belonged to me. Remember?"

I do remember that, strangely enough. My mouth quirks up in a half-smile. "I recall thinking you were a strangely possessive boy, yes. I'm glad we were friends."

Mathior's gaze is strangely intense as he toys with the end of my braid. "Did you think I jested, then?"

I gaze up at him, speechless. I'm having a hard time concentrating because of his nearness. He smells of sweat and horse and fresh air, and instead of that being appalling, it makes me long for the world outside. I like his scent. I know I should be thinking of other things than how he smells, but my goodness, when he stands this close, it's hard to think of anything but his presence. "I thought you were keeping me safe," I stammer. "As I kept you safe."

"I meant what I said. You belonged to me, even then. I've come to claim you."

4

HALLA

I stare at him in shock. The book tumbles from my grip and falls onto the floor, and still I cannot move.

"What do you mean?" I whisper. I can feel my cheeks turning scarlet even as fear tumbles through my belly. He's come to claim me. That can mean any number of things, given that the cyclops have so many different customs than my people. Perhaps he means that he will parade me through the streets in chains to show that I am subdued. After all, my father's father did such a thing with his enemies. But even as I speculate, I think of him touching my braid and my mind goes to...other things.

Like the picture in the book.

I've come to claim you.

Heat flutters in my belly. You silly spinster, I tell myself. Don't be like this. He is your enemy. You're his prisoner.

As I watch, Mathior leans over and picks up my book. He studies the cover and my heart slams in my throat. "Riekki's prayers?" He watches me carefully. "Have you taken up the vows of peace, then?"

Have I joined the temple's guardians? "No, not at all."

"Yet you read the prayers?" He gazes at the cover, and then opens the book, flipping through the pages.

And stops.

A slow smile curves his mouth as he gazes down at the drawing on the page.

Hot embarrassment scorches through me. I want to snatch the offending book out of his grip and toss it under my bunk, never to be seen again.

Mathior flicks a sly glance up at me. "I admit I've never followed Riekki's priesthood too closely, but I do not recall such things in my prayers."

I snatch the book away from him and clutch it to my breast. I don't want to know which picture he was looking at. I can imagine all kinds of embarrassments. "Tell me why you are here. Tell me what you want."

He laughs. "Can you not guess, lovely Halla?"

"Why you are here? Of course not." I hide behind my regal demeanor, even though my cheeks are flushed and my heart is pounding. "If you have not come to murder me and assure your claim on the throne, I don't know why you are here."

"I told you what I want."

Did I miss it somehow? "What?"

"You." The look he gives me is scorching.

Yet again, I am speechless. "King Mathior—"

"Call me Mathior. There is no need for titles between us."

I take a steeling breath and hold the book tighter. I'm no longer terrified; now I'm just confused. "You have my mind going in circles. I don't know what to think. I thought you were here...I thought..." I can't quite say the words.

"That I was here to destroy my rivals?" His mouth twists slightly. "It has been a long time since we have seen each other, but I have never thought unkindly of you. And I would never go back on my word."

You're safe because you're mine.

"You were a boy," I protest. "I don't expect—"

"My mind has not changed," he says, and his expression is so intense it steals the breath from my lungs. When he reaches out to capture my braid again, I tremble. "You're shaking. Sit."

A strong arm goes around my waist and he escorts me to the nearest bench. Of course, my knees get even weaker with his nearness, but I manage to sit down with a modicum of grace. I set the book carefully at my side—away from him—and straighten my ugly gray robe, wishing that it was one of the corseted, ornate Yshremi dresses I used to wear. Not because I loved them, but because they always made me feel regal and in control.

Mathior sits down next to me and studies my face. "I see my suggestion has shocked you."

"I don't understand," I tell him in a low voice. "Why—"

He raises a hand to quiet me. "You and I both know that there will never be peace in this kingdom while you live and I am on the throne."

My mouth goes dry again. I do know this. That's exactly why I thought he'd come here to kill me. "So your solution is to...take me as your concubine?" While I'm flattered at the suggestion, I don't see how it'll possibly work. The Yshremi people will be insulted that their once-queen has been pulled from exile at a peaceful temple to serve in the cyclops lord's bed. And as for me...well, I'm past the age that is considered young and nubile. I am thirty-three years. I should have been married when I was sixteen. No one wants a concubine that found her first gray hair yesterday, or whose breasts aren't quite as high and perky as they once were.

"My concubine? No. I mean to take you as my bride." And he stares at me so intently that I feel naked despite the gray wool of my robe. "Yshrem needs unity. What better way than to unite our two families? Such alliances are common, are they not?"

Between neighboring kingdoms, yes. Between conquered kingdom and conqueror, no. Between the wild cyclops tribes and my own rigid Yshremi people? Never. "You would do that to save my life?"

That slow, heart-stopping grin moves over his face again. "You mistake me yet again, Halla. I do not do this to save your life. I do this because you have always been destined to be mine." Mathior takes my hand in his and turns it over, then lifts it to his mouth. His tongue flicks over the center of my palm before he gives it a kiss. "I mean what I said. You are mine, Halla. I am king and I get what I want, and what I want is you. Yshrem can burn for all I care. Ask me to destroy it and I shall. Ask me to give it to you, and it will be yours...so long as you are in my bed."

The breath catches in my throat. "You...you want me?"

"Always." He brushes his mouth over the tips of my fingers. "Shall I show you how much?"

I am like a deer caught before the hunter. I cannot move, cannot protest...because I do not want to. I want him to show me exactly what he means, even though I know I should not. Just a short time ago I expected him to cut my throat. How can my world turn upside down so very quickly that I'm contemplating marriage? "But—"

Mathior snags one of my braids. The chosen hairstyle for Riekki's peacekeepers is two simple braids parted down the center of the head with one thick braid in the back. It's not an attractive hairstyle, but attractiveness doesn't matter when you are a deposed queen and spinster. But when he tugs on it and pulls me toward him, I feel pretty and irresistible. I feel his breath on my cheek a moment before his mouth closes over mine in a kiss.

I gasp and jerk backward, my eyes wide. The braid falls from his grip and I hold it tight against my collar, startled. I've never been kissed before. No one would dare to do such a thing without a royal engagement. Yet Mathior has been here for five minutes and already kissed me. I'm shocked...and fascinated.

This is as far from the quiet life in Riekki's temple as one can get.

The cyclops just grins at me, as if pleased by my shocked reaction. "Do I take liberties, Halla? I won't apologize."

"You can't take liberties," I tell him in a daze. "You are the king. Everything in the kingdom belongs to you, including me."

He grunts, apparently not pleased with my response. "You still have a choice. I would not leave you trapped in a situation you despise. I remember well how you saved my life, and I would not destroy yours. If you wish to stay here and live with Riekki's peacekeepers, you may. But you will have to take a new name. Word will be spread far and wide of Halla of Yshrem's unfortunate death to a coughing sickness. You will simply become one of the penitent, living your life in servitude to the goddess. If that is what you wish, I will not stand in your way." Mathior leans in and pulls my other braid into his hand, caressing it. "But if you wish to become mine, you should know of the cyclops marriage customs, because that is how we shall be wedded."

"Oh?" My voice is shaky, my head spinning. He's so close that I wonder if he's going to kiss me again. There's a heat throbbing between my thighs that I've only felt when I was alone and giving myself furtive, forbidden touches. I want his mouth on me again, no matter how impudent a gesture it was. "Tell me."

"My people's marriage ceremonies take place over three days."

That doesn't sound so bad. Yshremi unions can be long-winded and take hours, depending on how many priests of the different gods are involved. Every wedding has feasting and dancing, and if there is a union of two kingdoms, celebrations can go on for weeks as guests stream in to the city. I expected such things of my own wedding. "Three days," I echo. "Very well."

"The first day is the Revealing of the Bride to the groom. You will be presented in front of me and your clothing torn from your body. You will be displayed to all of those present so no flaws or defects can be hidden under clothing."

My eyes go wide. Stripped naked before court? It sounds like my worst nightmare. This is their wedding custom?

"On the second day of the ceremony, there is the Tasting of the Bride. You will be chaperoned so there is a witness that you find my caresses pleasing."

I frown at him, because I don't understand what he's saying. "Chaperoned for kissing?"

A wicked smile curves his mouth. "I said *tasting*, lovely Halla. My head will be between your thighs and I will taste you and you can determine if I am skilled enough to be your husband."

I swallow hard, utterly shocked, and I think of the picture in my book. Heat is flushing through my body again. By all the gods. I struggle to find something to say, and eventually reply with, "Oh. Well...well." My voice dies and I clear my throat. "And day three?"

"The Claiming of the Bride. I will take you as mine on that night." His gaze is heated. "Think on what I offer you. If you marry me, you must accept my people's ceremonies. To do otherwise would only fuel concerns that you are marrying me against your will. Make no mistake, I want you—but Yshrem needs peace." He gets to his feet before I can say anything. "I will return in the morning for your answer."

I stare blankly as he and his men stride out of the courtyard.

5

HALLA

*T*he Cyclopae wedding sounds utterly shocking.

I can't stop thinking about it as I lie in my pallet that night. Truth be told, I haven't been able to think of anything but Mathior since he left my side. I never expected to see him again. I certainly did not expect to see him as a grown man, savage and untamed, with a wicked grin that makes my pulse flutter.

He wants to marry me.

Not just because of Yshrem. Because he says he wants me. That he has always wanted me. I'm not sure what to think. I clutch my scratchy blankets to my chest and try to imagine what this means. If I choose to stay here in Riekki's temple, amongst her devoted, he will ensure that I am safe. I will give up my name, my past, my self entirely, and become just another temple devotee. I will live the rest of my days surrounded in gray.

Truly, it is not such a bad thing, I reason. Riekki's people have been kind.

But it is not me. I do not fit in here. Just because I have lived here peacefully for sixteen years does not mean I belong. I am not called to serve the goddess, and I feel like a pretender when I see the avid devotion on the faces of those around me.

Can I marry a cyclops warrior, though? I think of Mathior and the fearsome-looking eyepatch that covered half his face. I think of his fur cloak over his naked chest, and the weapons he wore strapped to his body. He is tall now, no longer a small boy. His body is graceful and lean, but corded with muscle. Any woman would be proud to call such a man hers. He's noble despite his wildness, and if the man is half as thoughtful as the boy, he will be a fine king.

And I am...old.

Thirty-three is not so old, not truly. But as far as virginal brides go, I am ancient. I am a spinster that should have been married off when I was young and fresh and had a throne to bring to my husband. Now I am no one and I have nothing to call my own save my face. Even the gray gown I wear belongs to the temple.

Well, that's not entirely true. I have a stash of dirty books.

I flush in the dark, thinking of Mathior's expression as he picked up the book and saw the drawing. He didn't look scandalized. He looked...interested. Intrigued. Aroused.

My breath quickens in my throat, and my hand steals under the blankets. I have the sudden urge to touch myself between my thighs, to rub that forbidden spot and feel my body tense up until I cannot stand it any longer. I imagine him as the picture, putting his tongue between my thighs and licking me, and a low groan escapes my throat.

Horrified, I clap a hand over my mouth and go silent, hoping that those sleeping in the nearby cells did not hear such a thing. No one gets up to check on me, though, and I relax.

I feel guilty, though. I should be thinking about Yshrem, about how I can benefit my people by being the wife of the king—no matter who the king is. I can bring about change if I have my husband's ear. Instead, all I am thinking about is what it would be like to kiss him, what it would be like for him to put his tongue in secret places.

Truly, I am a terrible person.

I worry, too. I can't sleep because when I close my eyes, I worry about the answer I will give in the morning. I want to say yes. Even if I found Mathior repulsive, I can do more to help my people as the wife to the king than simply hiding away in Riekki's temple for the rest of my days. But I am older than him. He is in his prime and must be all of twenty-four years now. I will be thirty-three in a month's time. He should get himself a bride who is young and sweet and will bring him an alliance. Instead, if I agree to marry him, he will be getting an older woman who has nothing but a useless family name and breasts that have not yet started to sag, but will soon enough.

He can do better. I know I have a pleasing face and I am well-versed in courtly manners, but so are a dozen other princesses half my age that would be thrilled to have such a handsome man as their husband. It does not matter that he is cyclops. Their ways are strange, but they are a strong tribe and devoted to the gods. There are worse choices to make, in my eyes.

I want to say yes...but I am terrified of what happens next. For the first time in sixteen years, I will leave the walls of Riekki's quiet temple and re-enter the world as Princess Halla of Yshrem. I will be betrothed to the man who conquered my kingdom and whose father killed my father on the field of battle. I will return with him to Yshrem, and then we will begin the marriage ceremony.

Three days, he said. Three ceremonies.

The Revealing of the Bride, where I will be stripped naked before the entire court. I break out into a cold sweat at the very thought. Even if I were in my prime marriageable years, I would be horrified at the thought. But it is a tradition, and it does not sound like Mathior will bend on such a request.

Of course, then there will be the Tasting of the Bride, which makes me even more nervous. He will put his mouth on me in front of a witness. I cannot imagine the reasoning behind such a thing, but I am both titillated and terrified of that.

The marriage bed itself almost seems like an afterthought. If I can get through day one and two of the wedding ceremony without fleeing, surely joining with my new husband will be a simple task.

Simple. Ha.

6

MATHIOR

*W*hen I return to the temple the next morning, I am as jittery as an unblooded warrior awaiting his first battle. Last night, I was certain that Halla would say yes to my demands. That no matter how she felt about me, she would give herself in marriage for Yshrem. But as the morning dawned, my certainty disappeared. Halla has never let anyone push her into anything. Even when her life was at stake, she remained firm and steadfast. It's one of the things I like so much about her.

If she does not wish to marry me, there is nothing I can say or do to convince her. I am king, of course. First Warrior of all the cyclops tribes and ruler of Yshrem and Adassia. If I demanded it, she would not be able to turn me down. But I want her in my bed of her own free will, not because I have forced her there. I do not mind a shy bride.

I am no rapist to force a woman to my bed, though. If she says no, it will be no. No matter how badly I want her.

And I do want her quite badly.

Sixteen years had passed since I saw her last. I wondered if she had grown old and withered, or if my child's mind had made her out to be more graceful and beautiful than she truly was. Even the drab clothing and braids of Riekki's peacekeepers could not hide her loveliness, though. She is just as I remembered—her face a beautiful oval dominated by wide, long-lashed eyes and a full pink mouth. Her body is more womanly than I remember, her breasts straining against the fabric of the gray robe. Her face is unlined and sweet, and she looks as untouched as she was over sixteen years ago.

No, I am not displeased with my choice to marry her. I wonder if she is displeased with me, though. I am burned brown by days in the sun, unlike the scholarly men of her country. I have battle scars of many fights, and I gave my left eye to the god years ago. I am very different from the boy she remembers. Her eyes went wide when she realized who I was, but she did not retreat, and that pleased me.

I hope she shows such fearlessness again today.

I stride into the temple the next morning, my cloak of office heavy around my shoulders. I have been told that Halla will see me in the courtyard once more, so I made my warriors wait outside. If Halla is shy or has questions, I want her to ask them freely.

Mostly I just want to kiss her again. Perhaps she will let me if others are not staring us down.

When I enter the courtyard, she is there, waiting. This time she has no naughty book in her lap, her hands clasped there instead. Her braids are carefully arranged over her shoulders and her expression is calm, her poise regal. She looks every bit the queen she was, despite the dull gray of her clothing. Her cheeks go pink at the sight of me, and I cannot stop grinning to myself.

She will say yes. That blush tells me everything.

I sit down across from her, in the empty chair that has been pulled next to hers. She does not fidget, my bride-to-be. She watches me calmly, her expression serene.

"Have you decided?" I ask, my words bald. I see no point in dancing around the reason for my visit.

Her cheeks pink again. "You can do better than me, my lord."

"Better?" I echo. "Better at what?"

Halla's flush deepens. "You know what I mean. Younger. Prettier. With more land or money. I have nothing anymore, my lord, not even a throne. I come to you with nothing but the robe on my back, and even that is given to me by the grace of the peace-keepers."

"Ah." I lean forward and take her hand in mine. She looks startled, but I do not let her go. "So you think I am choosing poorly for my bride."

She hesitates.

"Will it help if I tell you that ever since I became a man, it was the memory of your face I stroked my cock to when I lay in my bed at night?" I hear her sudden intake of breath and the shocked look on her face, but I don't let go of her hand. "Will it ease your fears to know it is you I have always wanted?"

Halla's mouth works silently, that pink softness just begging for another kiss. I want to lean in and taste her again, but she speaks before I can. "I am old, Mathior."

I snort. "You are not old. You are barely three and thirty, if I remember your birth-date correctly."

"And you are twenty-three—"

"Twenty-four," I correct. "And I have female warriors in my tribe that are twice your age and still as hale as any."

"I'm a spinster," she continues stubbornly, ignoring my words. "Even if I had a kingdom, there are younger princesses, or those that have proven to be childbearers. What if I am too old to provide you with an heir?"

Is that truly her only worry? Or just an argument because she is afraid? "Then my strongest warrior will take my place as First Warrior. It is the cyclops way. I would not have followed my father to the throne if I were not the most capable in all of my tribe."

"But—"

"I will have you," I tell her firmly. "As my bride and in my bed. Are excuses all that you have for me? Or do you truly not want to be my wife? Say so now. I would not force an unwilling woman."

Her cheeks color prettily again and for the first time, her hand twitches in mine. "I will marry you." Her voice is a shy whisper. "But Mathior—"

"No buts. You will marry me in the cyclops way?"

Halla lifts her chin. "You ask permission to strip me naked in front of your people and mine, put your mouth on me"—her face becomes redder, which I did not know was possible—"and then bed me? If that is what it takes to unify our people, I shall do so gladly."

"Do you marry me only to unify your people, then?"

For a moment, she looks confused. She straightens and that soft mouth presses into a line. "I do not understand what you ask, Mathior."

I straighten and release her hand. "Kiss me." I want to see how she will respond to caresses. Nothing will be more disappointing than dreaming of Halla for sixteen years only to find she is repulsed by the touch of a cyclops. Her people think of us as crude barbarians, fools who carve up their faces in a show of strength. She will willingly submit to me...but how willingly? Perhaps I am overly prideful in this moment, but I want more than just her reluctance.

I want her passion as I have dreamed it for all these years.

Halla looks around the room, then when she sees no one else, turns her startled gaze to me. "Kiss you, my lord?"

"Mathior," I demand. "Call me by my name. I want to hear it from your lips."

"Mathior," she murmurs, and bites one full, pink lip. "Forgive me. I just...protocol..."

"Protocol has nothing to do with the two of us," I tell her. "If I were a king that believed in protocol, I would do as you think I should and marry some royal daughter with lineage and money and not a thought in her head. I want you. I have always wanted you. I cannot make that any clearer. So if you wish to marry me, come and give me a kiss."

She looks frustrated at my demands. "It's not that easy—"

"It is just a kiss. Nothing more. I will not bear you down into the rushes and have my way with you."

Yet.

Halla makes the most adorably indignant sound, and then gets to her feet. "Very well." She smooths her skirts and waits.

I don't get up from my seat. I pat my thigh and lean back, giving her an expectant look.

Her nostrils flare, the only outward sign of her frustration. She gazes at me for a long moment, and I half-expect her to storm away. Instead, she moves forward and with all the grace of the princess she is, sits on my knee. She's tiny, I realize, her weight light. She fits into my arms perfectly, though, and it takes everything I have not to wrap my arms around her and drag her against me.

I want to see how she handles this.

Halla moves ever so slightly inward, studying me. Then she leans in and puts her mouth against mine. The movement is quick, firm.

Abrupt.

I don't react.

She hesitates and her mouth remains against mine. I can feel the press of her body against my chest, and her hands stray to my skin. Her fingertips rest against my pectoral and her lips move hesitantly, parting against mine.

Then, she pulls back. "I don't know what I'm doing," she admits softly.

I bite back the groan that rises in my throat. She is untouched, and it fills me with a fierce possessive pleasure. "Shall I show you?"

"Please."

I slide my hand along her back and let it rest on her hip. She stiffens against me but doesn't move away. My other hand goes to her hair and I pull her back down until her mouth grazes over mine. I part my lips, letting her feel my mouth before I flick my tongue against the part of her lips. "Open for me."

She gasps, but does as I command.

I slide my tongue into her mouth, and she immediately goes pliant against me. A little noise of pleasure escapes her, and my cock hardens at the realization that she enjoys my touch. She thinks she is a spinster? Not in my arms. I stroke against her tongue, licking at her sweetness and tasting her as I have always dreamed. Halla's hand curls against my chest and her nails dig into my skin, and again the fierce, possessive pride ripples through me.

It does not matter that she is older than me. She is mine and mine alone. With that thought, I growl low in my throat and deepen the kiss, claiming her mouth with deep, sure strokes. To my surprise—and pleasure—Halla timidly returns the kisses, her tongue brushing against mine. For all that she is unschooled, she is not cold.

This pleases me greatly. I have kissed only a very few females, and always with her foremost in my mind. Every cyclops male is trained to please a female in bed, but I have never claimed one as my own. I have been waiting for my Halla, and the kisses I give her now are a result of learning what it will take to pleasure a female.

Not just any female, but mine.

So I nibble on her mouth, on those full, pink lips, before stroking deep once more. When she makes another soft whimper and her hand curls against my chest, I gentle my kiss, turning it to one of exploration and languid pleasure. There will be time enough to plunder her, I reason with myself. I must go slow. I must be gentle. So I lap at her mouth, flicking my tongue against hers until she squirms with pleasure, and the nipples rubbing against my chest are hard little beads that make my cock surge with aching need.

I would bear her to the floor and claim her as mine right now if I were not king. But I am, and she is a princess of the Yshrem line, and what we do must be public so all will know we are united. With a sigh, I pull away from the soft sweetness of her mouth and give her one final nip. "Say you will be mine, Halla."

She gives me a dazed, passion-glazed look, her focus on my mouth. "Of course, my lord."

"Mathior. Always Mathior to you."

A smile touches her kiss-swollen lips. "Mathior."

It takes everything I have not to claim her mouth as mine again. I gently set her onto her feet and then get to my own. My cock throbs under my loincloth, but I ignore it and the obvious bulge it makes. "When can you be ready to leave?"

She straightens her clothes and runs a trembling hand over her braids. "I do not have much, so I could be ready in an hour. However, if you want to marry a princess, I shouldn't leave the temple dressed like a peacekeeper. Send your men out to get me a dress fit for a queen, and a horse of my own, and we can ride out in the morning where everyone can see us coming up the roads."

I'm amused at how quickly her manner changed from sweetly giving and unsure to brisk and efficient. This is the Halla I remembered—a queen down to her bones. She is right. It has been sixteen years since any saw their princess. For them to recognize her as such, she will need to be garbed in the manner befitting a queen. If I take her out of here in the plain spun robe she is currently wearing, they will think I have snatched her. I'm both pleased and amused at her clever mind. "It shall be done. I'll have a dress delivered this afternoon."

"You have the banns?"

"Banns?" I stare at her blankly.

"Banns," she agrees. "A Yshremi custom. The bride and groom travel the streets with a banner showing the house symbols that will be united. It's so the common people can come out and receive blessing coins." She lifts her chin. "You should probably go to the nearest moneylender as well and take out a great many coins. You wouldn't want to look poor in front of my people."

So because I am marrying her in my custom, I am also to marry her in hers? Impudent to suggest, but wise, too. I grin. "It shall be done. My house has no symbol, though. That is a Yshremi custom."

"You'll think of something," she says coolly, and straightens. "I must go and inform the peacekeepers that I will be leaving. Will you compensate them for my care for all these years?"

"Of course. You are quick to spend my money," I tease.

"You're marrying a princess," she tells me in a tart voice as she saunters away. "We are not cheap."

I throw back my head and laugh with delight.

I HAVE a dress sent to the temple later that evening, and when I arrive with my warriors the next morning, we bring a pale gray mare for her to ride upon. Since we ride to the capital with all of my tribe, hundreds of Cyclopae warriors fill the streets, and it is easy to tell the Yshremi local people are alarmed. Families hide away at the sight of the crossed spears on our backs and the eyepatches on our faces. They probably think we are here to conquer once more.

Halla was wise to suggest the banns and the dress. Two bags of coins are tied to my horse's saddle and a bag tied to her mare. I have given my men equal amounts of the Yshremi coins so they can also toss them at the people. If all it takes is a few coins to make them forget our spears, then it is a small price indeed.

The gates of the temple open in silence, and Halla meets us on the steps. One of the peacekeepers holds a small bag in her arms, but Halla herself is as regal and lovely as I remember. The dress I chose for her is a bright, fiery red, trimmed with white fur. It will stand out like a lightning bolt against the mare. She will be impossible to miss. Her hair is braided in a coronet that makes her look regal and elegant even without a circlet for her brow. I approach and offer her my hand.

She comes down the steps and puts her hand lightly on mine. "Did you get the banns?"

I turn and gesture at the men riding at the front of my warriors. Two long, fluttering flags are unraveled, and the symbol of House Yshrem—a scroll—is next to the symbol I have created for my people. It is an eye with a red handprint over it, symbolizing both my cyclops people and our love of battle.

Once the banns unfurl, a cheer goes up around us and I turn. I did not realize we had an audience, but people have streamed out of their homes, and as Halla strides forward, they continue to call out her name. She is well loved here.

She will be well loved by me, as well. I am pleased.

_____

7

HALLA

*C*astle Yshrem looks just as I remember it.

I stare up at the stone walls as I am escorted inside. The sounds of cheering have followed me all through the streets for the last few days. I'm just happy the sounds are pleased ones instead of terrified ones. The sight of cyclops warriors riding through the villages and towns of Yshrem is a fearsome one and reminds people of the conquest sixteen years ago. The moment they see me—and the banners of marriage—their fear turns to excitement. They feel safe in their own home again.

If nothing else, my marriage will give my people that.

So I am glad for it. I do not mind the long days in the saddle as we ride to the capital, or that my arm aches from waving at those who crowd near our horses, curious about their barbarian king and his bride. Mathior has spent a fortune in bridal coins these last three days of travel, but he has not complained, and this makes me happy. I'm happy that my husband will be a king who realizes that content, happy people are the best kinds of subjects.

My husband.

I stare up at the banners on the stone walls. Whoever was sent ahead to prepare the castle has done fast work. The marriage banns hang from every wall, his symbol next to mine as far as the eye can see. Once we are inside the gates, he and his men split off, though, and I'm surrounded by ladies and housekeepers who bow obeisance and then have a dozen questions for me. They are clearly flustered, not certain of their place or what is going on. I know how that feels. Watching Mathior and the other cyclops guards leave me behind...that was not a good feeling.

But I know how to handle myself in uncomfortable situations. I am no wilting flower. I straighten my shoulders and gaze at the women evenly and hand out tasks even as I glean information from them. The women—young Yshremi ladies or wives of the garrison soldiers—look relieved that someone else is in charge, and I sweep through the castle, noting the changes since I last saw it sixteen years ago.

I am told that a local Yshremi lordling who bowed the knee at King Alistair has lived here ever since the conquest. He ruled this area in exchange for sending horses and an ungodly amount of taxes to the cyclops king. A traitor to his people in exchange for his own favor, I think, but I do not say such things aloud. I know very well the type of men that were rewarded when Yshrem fell to Alistair. I am also told that when the lordling received news of our arrival, he fled in the night. I suspect that perhaps someone was not paying his taxes as he should, and I feel a very un-royal bit of glee at that.

The keep itself is dirty and in disrepair despite the fact it has been held by Yshremi hands all this time. I give the housekeepers orders, discuss ways to house all of the cyclops warriors that are traveling with my soon-to-be-husband, and then talk of the upcoming marriage.

They look terrified on my behalf, though do not dare speak up and say so. Strangely enough, I'm not afraid. Intimidated by what is to come, yes, but I think of Mathior and his mouth on mine, and his boyish smile of pleasure when he sees me, and I feel a flush of pleasure.

There will be three days of ceremonies, I explain to the ladies and housekeepers that surround me. Each day will require a feast in the throne room for the cyclops warriors. I send a messenger out to the nearest lordlings, since it will not hurt to have our nuptials witnessed by Yshremi eyes. The sooner the word spreads of our union, the better.

One timid woman—one of the old lordling's cousins, I think—clutches the fur muff in her hands and gives me a worried look. "How long will the cyclops be visiting?" she asks, her voice low and hushed.

"Visiting?" I inquire.

"Yes. How long before they leave once more?"

I gaze at the women, all wide-eyed and worried. I don't blame them for being fearful—we've all heard terrible stories of the ruthlessness of cyclops warriors. We've seen their ruthlessness ourselves when our kingdom was conquered. Perhaps they expect the cyclops to ride in, destroy everything as they did before, and then, like sixteen years ago, ride away and return to their hunting grounds.

It occurs to me that I don't know Mathior's plans, either. Perhaps his idea all along has been to install me as ruler and wife to quell the surges of uprising, and then ride away with his men once the wedding has finished. I should be pleased at the idea of being on my own to rule, but I find the idea...disappointing.

"I shall ask this evening," I reassure her.

I DO NOT SEE Mathior for the rest of the day, but the keep is crawling with cyclops warriors. They stand out amongst the pale, heavily robed Yshremi people with their bare chests and bronze skin and the weapons crossed over their backs. It seems that even in a peaceful keep, they are armed to the teeth. They are everywhere, too—walking the castle walls, in the courtyard, practicing sparring out in the fields. One follows behind me at all times, and I suspect that Mathior is having me guarded. I don't mind that—it's to be expected. But when I try to ask him questions, he just stares at me in silence.

Eventually I retire to my chambers and send a lady out with a note for my guard, asking him to find Mathior and invite him to dinner in my quarters this evening. I don't know if he'll show up, but it seems worth a try. I have a table set out with food and drink and wait patiently in my chair. The chamber I'm in is my old one from so many years ago, though the furniture is new and so are the rugs. I try not to dwell on the past, but it is difficult.

Mathior arrives a short time after dark, and I'm surprised to see that he is not alone. Three warriors have accompanied him, and as he enters my chambers and takes off his white fur cloak, the men line up against the wall and wait by the door.

"Is there a problem?" I ask as Mathior thumps down into the chair across from mine at the table.

"Problem?" he asks, filling a cup with wine and taking a large gulp of it. He drinks deeply and then leans back, sighing, as if he's had a long day. I notice he's a little sweaty, his long hair damp on the one side, and I feel suddenly nervous. My palms grow moist and my heart pounds because when he drinks again, he watches me over the brim of his cup.

"You have armed guards with you. Do you expect trouble?" I arch a brow. "Or do you expect me to assassinate you?"

He throws his head back and laughs. "I think you could not harm a flea, my lovely Halla."

"Then what is it?"

Mathior sets down his cup and leans forward, giving me a sly grin. "We are not yet wedded. They are here to chaperone us, as is custom. Until I have claimed you as my wife, we cannot be alone together."

Heat scalds my cheeks. "I see." I pick up my own cup and take a long drink, because I need a bit of courage after hearing that. His words—and the sexy tone he says them in—make me think of the upcoming wedding. I force myself to relax, to keep my tone neutral as I set down my cup. "I've let the housekeepers know that there will be a wedding ceremony. Just let me know when you would like to—"

"Tomorrow." His one eye gleams with a possessive light as he takes another drink. "We begin tomorrow with the Revealing of the Bride."

"Very well," I say faintly. Tomorrow I will be stripped naked before the court and offered to him like a barbarian slave girl. I'm both horrified and aroused at the thought. Shifting in my seat to ease the throbbing between my thighs, I toy with my cup. "How long will you remain in Yshrem after the ceremony?"

His gaze narrows. "What do you mean?"

I fear I've offended him. The eve before my wedding is not the time to anger my conquering bridegroom, and I feel a shiver of worry skitter down my spine. I lick my lips and compose myself. "Your father did not remain in Yshrem. Your people are a nomadic one, are they not? The hunting lands are not impressive here. We are a cultivated country with fields and not forests. I am merely curious how long you will remain in Yshrem for the wedding before you and your men leave to return to your homelands."

Mathior gets to his feet. Everything inside me clenches, and I worry I've said or done something so offensive that he's going to leave. I open my mouth to protest, but as I watch, he heads toward the shuttered window instead, and my fears die in my throat. He pushes open the casement shutters and then looks over at me, gesturing out. "Come and tell me what you see."

I rise and move to his side, my skirts swishing over the stone floors. "It's dark outside."

"Not so very dark," he tells me. "Come and look anyhow."

I do, peering out the window. My chambers are high up in the keep itself, so I have a good view of the castle surroundings. The courtyard below has the usual shuffle of servants and guards heading back and forth on their tasks, the stables full this time of night. Torches flicker on the battlements. I don't see anything out of the ordinary, so I look farther. Outside of the castle walls themselves, I see dark shapes dotting the ground, and campfires. Horses wander between the shapes and I realize the triangular dark shapes are tents. The cyclops warriors have chosen to stay outside of the castle walls. "What does this mean?"

"Mean?" he asks, brow furrowing.

"They do not stay within the gates of Castle Yshrem? Is that what you wished for me to see?"

Mathior chuckles. "They do not stay within because they choose to be near their horses, nothing more. No, I wished for you to see that they set up tents." He gives me an amused look, as if this explains everything.

I'm even more confused than before, though. "And?"

"And a cyclops does not set up a home unless he is staying for a time. He will sleep under the stars if he will journey onward shortly." He reaches out and touches the long singular braid I have over my shoulder. My hair is so long and thick that I don't want to leave it loose like the cyclops do, but one of the ornate braids of my people seems uncompromising. So I tied it into a simple, loose braid over one shoulder. As he touches it, I'm oddly glad that I did such a small thing. He likes my hair, and it fills me with pleasure at such a small realization. It takes me a moment to realize he is still speaking, even as he touches my braid. "My men and I are staying."

"You are?" I cannot help but be surprised. "In Yshrem?"

"For a time, yes." He doesn't let go of my braid, thoughtfully rubbing the tail of it between his thumb and forefinger as he gazes out the window. "It's clear to me that my father was wrong in many of his choices. I will not say he was wrong to conquer this place"—and he flashes me a grin—"but he was wrong to ignore it in favor of his own preferences. A good king must see to all his people, and now that it is mine, I must see to its well-being as much as any cyclops lands."

I'm impressed by his thoughts. He seems young to me, but his words are wise. "I can rule from here if you are needed elsewhere."

Mathior turns back to me, and he gives my braid a little tug. "I did not say you would be left behind, sweet Halla. I've waited sixteen years to claim you. I'm not letting you slip from my grasp again."

It shouldn't matter, but I still feel warm at his words. "So how long will we stay, then?"

"Until I am convinced things are settled. Months. Maybe a year. I don't know for sure. Then we will go to Adassia and settle things there. Then we will return to Cyclopae for a time. Then we will likely do it all once more."

It makes sense. I gaze out at the sea of tents around the castle. Adassia is more like Yshrem than Cyclopae. They will be giving up much to be leaving their families and familiar hunting grounds for such a long time. "There is much unrest in both Adassia and Yshrem," I admit to him. I heard terrible things every day when in the temple. "What if there is no peaceful solution?"

He chuckles and tweaks my braid again. "My love, we are a warrior people. There is nothing my men would like more than a good battle."

I stare up at him, shocked. Did he just call me his love?

"You heard right," Mathior says quietly. He slowly wraps my braid around his hand with a motion of his wrist and pulls me forward. "Did you think I lied when I said I had waited for you sixteen years?" He twines my braid tighter, until I am standing practically against him.

He leans in, dark hair spilling over one shoulder, his lone eye gleaming in the candlelight, and I realize he is going to kiss me again. It shocks me to think that he loves me...almost as much as the realization that I want him to kiss me again, very much. I should hate him and all his people for conquering mine. I should loathe him because his father killed my father.

But...I am not my father. And Mathior is not his.

And I still want to be kissed.

Mathior's breath fans over my face, and my entire body tingles in response, full of anticipation.

Across the room, a throat is gently cleared. One of the guards.

Mathior goes still, and then he grimaces. He releases my braid and straightens. "Three days. I will not dishonor you before then." He glances over at the guards, then back at me. "But I will be thinking about it. A lot."

I can't help but blush at that. I'm going to be thinking about it, too.

8

HALLA

*T*he next day, I'm kept entirely sequestered. The housekeepers flutter in and out of my chambers to give me updates on the feast that's being prepared, but other than that, I'm left alone. I will be called for, I'm told, when the king is ready to receive me. The royal part of my mind is utterly irritated that I have to be summoned like I'm no one, but this is part of the ritual of the cyclops wedding, and I did agree to be married in the manner of his people.

So I keep my small irritations to myself and try to hide the nervousness that has infected every inch of my body.

I call for a bath early in the afternoon, and the ladies assigned to me scrub and perfume every inch of my skin. Every stray hair is removed from my body until I am completely smooth save between my thighs, which is left natural, and then I am lotioned and oiled until my pale skin glistens. My hair is a mixture of Yshremi and Cyclopae styles—I wear a delicate coronet of braids encircling my brow, a ribbon woven through the plaits. The rest of my hair is left free to cascade down my back in a curly fall.

And then I obsess over my clothing.

What does one wear to a public disrobing? As women bring in gowns fit for a queen, it's clear that one of the local tailors has been told that I have returned, because several of the dresses are in the pale lavender color of my father's household. I touch one absently, thinking of my stately father.

He'd always wanted me to marry a king. I can't imagine what he would think of such a wedding, or the fact that I'm going to be stark naked in front of the entire court in a few short hours.

I'm not thinking about what comes after this. One day at a time.

I can hear people below, the murmur of voices in the throne room that drifts up to my window, and I feel another shiver of nervous anticipation. They will call for me soon. Last night, Mathior explained that he would take his throne, tell the gathered nobles of his plans to retake Yshrem, and then would bring me out for the ceremony. After the "revealing," I will have the choice to stay for the public feast celebrating the marriage festivities, or I can choose to retire to my chambers. I cannot spend time alone with him until we are wedded.

I should be present at the feast, but I'm not even sure that a princess trained from birth to be a ruler can calmly sit in front of the people she was naked before just a short time ago. Far better for me to retreat to my rooms and compose myself.

One of the ladies arrives with my corset and pantaloons, and they are lacy, frothy things of the same pale purple as my dress. I can feel myself blushing at the thought of Mathior seeing these...and everyone else will, too. Oh, gods. For a moment, I feel as if I am going to be sick.

But I chose this. I promised to wed him willingly. And I think of Mathior and how he will look at me. The sick clench in my gut eases, leaving nothing more than nervous anticipation. My corset is tightened and laced, and then my dress is slipped over my head. The long sleeves are adjusted, and the sides are laced tight to show off my still-becoming figure. A decorative belt is slung over my hips, and my hair is smoothed and adjusted until it falls perfectly over my shoulders. I wish I had my mother's jewelry, but it is long gone, paid to the Cyclopae in Yshrem's conquest and was likely melted down long ago.

There is a brisk knock at my door.

The girl serving me looks pleased. "Are you ready, my lady? A public wedding ceremony is so exciting."

She is Yshremi. I doubt she knows how truly "exciting" tonight shall be. "I am ready," I say in my calmest voice. "Let us be on our way."

When we open the door, though, I am surprised to see that the Cyclopae guards waiting there for me are women. Both are dressed as the men, with leather breeches and nothing but a leather harness over their breasts. Each bears only one eye and the eyepatch of a blooded Cyclops warrior, and they look just as fierce as their brethren.

"First Warrior Mathior has sent us to retrieve his bride for the Revealing," one says, and I think she must be about my age. "Follow us."

I nod and pick up my skirts, feigning a calmness I do not feel. "You are women that serve as warriors," I comment as we descend the stairs and they flank me, my maid fluttering behind me and fussing with my skirts. "Have you never had a marriage ceremony, then?" I wonder if I am the only one "lucky" enough to be married in such a manner.

"I have," the one to my left says. She smiles, and it takes some of the hardness off of her expression. "Stood proudly in front of my husband and the entire tribe wearing nothing but a smile. I had nothing to hide."

"And do the men undress for us?" I ask, since it is clear both men and women can be warriors. Why not?

Both women only laugh as if I have said something utterly hilarious. "Are you going to ask First Warrior to disrobe for you, then? So you can see what he brings to the marriage?" the other asks.

"I just might," I say mildly. Not every warrior carries a sword. I can be just as strong and fierce as these ladies, if I must. And I am just as royal as Mathior is.

This only makes them laugh more. "I should like to see that," the married one says with a wink.

But then we are at the doors that lead into the great hall, and I can see people lining the long room. There are Cyclopae warriors mixed with the more modestly dressed people of my kingdom. And there are a great many people. So many that the moment we enter the chamber, a wall of heat hits us from the press of bodies. The air is thick and heavy, and everything goes silent when I enter.

At the front of the crowded chamber, Mathior sits on the dais. I remember my father had a jeweled throne of ornate wood inlaid with gold and lapis. The barbarian who rules Yshrem now cares for no such niceties. His chair is a simple one, with no back and two wooden arm rests. If I did not know better, I would swear it was a camp stool, but he makes it look intimidating. He leans forward on his "throne," as if impatient with court and ready to be done with the niceties. Though this is court proper, he wears the same clothing he always does—leather breeches, the white fur cloak of First Warrior, and his hair flows long over one shoulder. One eye is covered in the crude eyepatch he always wears, but it does not detract from the sight of him.

He's so handsome it takes my breath away.

Mathior's gaze lights on me the moment I enter, and he gets to his feet. A hint of a smile curves his hard mouth. "People of Yshrem. My Cyclopae warriors. You know that I come to this land with one intention—to bring unity to our peoples. When a kingdom's people feel safe, it is when they are happiest. You look upon my warriors and you do not feel pride at the sight of them. You feel fear. Unease. And we have done nothing to change that." He gazes out on the people gathered before him, and he truly looks like a king despite his youthful age. I'm pleased. He continues. "I know that for many, many years, safety is not something that the land of Yshrem has felt. I mean to change that in many ways, starting now."

People clap politely, but I can see the eagerness on their faces. They are waiting to hear my name. They want to hear of the royal wedding. I can feel another shiver of distress move through my body and my nipples grow hard against my corset. Gods, I hope that passes before I am stripped naked.

Just as I hope no one can see that my pantaloons will be damp between the thighs.

Mathior descends the steps of the dais slowly.

One.

Two.

Three.

He approaches but doesn't come close. The women at my side don't move, either. Me, I'm scarcely breathing, my gaze locked upon the man who seems to be taking up all the space in this room. It doesn't matter that the entire chamber is full of Yshremi and Cyclopae alike—all I can see before me is Mathior.

"In the name of unity, I have decided to take a bride," he calls out. He glances around the room, but then his gaze swings back to me and pins me in place. "Princess Halla of Yshrem has agreed to be married in the custom of my people. Is that not so?"

He turns to me, and I wonder if I am supposed to kneel. We did not go over the details of the ceremony, and now I wish we had. He may be the ruler, but if we are to be seen as a union, me bowing before him like a mewling, downtrodden waif begging for mercy—for all that I am—will not endear my people to him.

So I step forward and extend my hand for him to take, a gracious smile on my face.

Someone coughs, and I wonder if it is another one of those warnings from his guards. The room is very still despite the humid air, and I can hear a low whisper somewhere in the back. The moment seems to hang forever.

Mathior takes my hand, then tucks it into the crook of his arm. "Let us begin the ceremony of the Revealing of the Bride."

Perhaps I'm not to be stripped naked after all. Relief, hot and profound, moves over me, and I smile brilliantly up at Mathior. He grins down at me, and then begins to walk along the room, near the edge of the crowd. A cyclops warrior slaps his hand on his thigh, and then another, and then it seems as if the whole room is slapping in time to a stately, ominous beat as Mathior parades me about.

It's a quick turn, and then his hand covers mine, giving it a squeeze before moving back to the center of the hall and releasing me. I realize in that moment that this isn't the end of things after all. That nervous, strange heat pools in my belly once more as I go to stand between the female guards and Mathior takes his place on the dais again. The slapping has not stopped. If anything, it only thunders louder and louder in my ears.

Mathior sits and the slapping stops. He gazes about the room and then calls out, "Have all seen my bride and judged her fair?"

"Aye," returns a chorus of Cyclopae voices.

His gaze moves back to me. "Then display her before her groom and the gods," he booms out in a shout.

There's a wild cheer even as the two women at my side grab my sleeves and rip the fabric.

I remain perfectly still, determined not to show any emotion. Several of the Yshremi people on the sidelines look startled as the two female warriors gleefully attack my clothing, shredding my pale lavender dress as the Cyclopae cheer so loud that it feels as if the entire room is shaking with the sound of it.

One sleeve is flung to the floor. Then the other.

The laces at my sides are torn away, and my belt is hacked from my waist with a knife. All the while, I remain still, and Mathior's gaze is upon mine. The woman at my left takes a handful of the fabric on my shoulder, and then rips downward. I can hear gasps as my dress falls away and then I am in nothing but my corset and pantaloons. I can feel my breasts heaving, my breath panting in both terror and exhilaration.

I don't know why I feel this spiraling, wild glee inside me. Perhaps it's the way Mathior looks at me as each bit of clothing falls away, the look on his face more intense and full of need. I've never been looked at like that, ever. He stares at me as if I am his next breath of air, and I am dizzy with the wanting of him.

"I'm going to undo your corset now, my lady," one woman murmurs.

"I'm ready," I tell her. I don't look at the faces of the people in the audience, because if I do, I'll collapse. I keep my attention locked on Mathior and his intense, intent face.

"You are very brave, princess," the woman says, and then I feel the pop of the laces as her knife cuts through. A few more slices, and my corset falls away. My breasts bounce, free, and then my pantaloons are torn from my body.

I'm naked in front of the court. Completely naked, wearing nothing but my hair. I remain perfectly still as the Cyclops warriors break into fierce cheers, as if seeing my breasts is something to be proud of. I hope no one notices that my stomach isn't as flat as it was sixteen years ago, or my thighs have a little more jiggle. My breasts are full, and I lift my chin proudly as Mathior gets to his feet.

The hungry look is in his gaze as he approaches, and my nipples prick in response as he grows nearer. I'm panting. I want to stop, but I can't. It's like we're alone in the room and I'm presenting myself to him, and it's the most arousing and terrifying thing I've ever felt. He paces forward like a hungry lion and then circles around me. After a moment, he returns to stand in front of me, and a slow smile curves his mouth.

"I find my bride pleasing," he says in a loud, firm voice, and then takes the white fur cloak off his shoulders and tosses it over mine, hiding me from view.

More cheers erupt in the hall, and I clutch the fur cloak to my body as I gaze at him. I did it. I didn't collapse, though my knees feel dangerously close to doing so now. But I remember the conversation from earlier with the female warriors, and something in me cannot resist asking. I lift my chin higher and give my husband-to-be a lofty look. "Is it your turn now?"

One of the women at my side muffles a snort. Someone in the hall catcalls and jeers. Someone else gasps. There's a low murmur of whispers. I'm curious how Mathior will handle it. If he grows angry, I will know what kind of temper my future husband will have, at the very least.

But that wicked grin on his face just grows wider, and then he unbuckles his belt. His gaze remains locked on mine as he removes his belt, flings it to the floor, and then drops his pants.

"Do you find me pleasing, Halla?"

I doubt anyone could hear my response over the roar in the hall.

9

MATHIOR

*M*y little bride is brave. I think of it all through the first of the three feasts, which she does not attend. Her ladies—both Yshremi and Cyclopae—usher her away wearing nothing but my cloak, and that is the last I see of her. All night, people drink and slap me on the back to tell me what a fine bride I have.

I know this. I have always known this.

I'm stunned by her beauty, though. Her skin is as creamy as I've dreamt it would be. Her breasts are still high and proud, full, with dark pink nipples that just beg for a warrior's mouth. Her hips flared gently out to delicious pale thighs and a patch of dark curls over her cunt that makes my mouth water to think of. Most of all, though, I think of the proud, arrogant tilt of her head and the way she demanded the same of me.

I love that. I love how fearless she is. And I love that when she gazed upon my cock, her cheeks flamed bright red and her voice wobbled as she declared me pleasing to her as well.

My bride. My beautiful Halla. I am so close to making her mine.

The next day passes incredibly slowly. I am hungry for the next day's marriage ceremony, but it will not be held until that evening. I cannot sleep, because Halla haunts my dreams. I cannot spar with my men, because I cannot focus long enough to fight properly. This only makes my warriors laugh; they make crude jokes and tease me endlessly. After a few rounds of this, I give up and return to my audience chambers. I listen to advisors as they drone on and on about crops and trade routes and levies until I want to hit something. This, too, is part of being king, though, so I force myself to pay attention and take in all the advice given to me.

Eventually, though, darkness falls and people gather for the feast. I cannot be the first to arrive, lest I seem too eager. I am still king, for all that I am bridegroom as well. I dress for the feast, and when enough time has passed, I enter the feast hall.

A loud cheer goes up, and I raise a hand to silence them. I am pleased to see that both Yshremi and Cyclops are cheering. There is nothing quite like a wedding and feast to bring people together, it seems. Perhaps I should marry off more cyclops warriors to Yshremi brides. It's an intriguing concept and one I plan on discussing with Halla once I am alone with her.

Not tonight, though. Tonight, I plan on doing many other things with my bride. Tonight is the tasting, and my mouth waters with the thought of it.

The great hall has tables laid out, and people sit along the benches, waiting for the feast to begin. I move to my throne, still on the dais, and sit there impatiently, waiting for my bride. The food is served, dish after dish, drinking horn after drinking horn, but no one eats or drinks. As custom, no one can celebrate the "tasting" until we do.

Halla arrives in a sweep of lavender skirts a short time later, and the cheer goes up once more. I can tell even as she approaches that she is embarrassed, her shoulders stiff and regal. She keeps a gracious smile on her face as people call out ribald jokes. Only during a wedding are such things allowed. Once the three days have passed, we will be king and queen and the rules of court will return once more. But for now, the excitement of a wedding and feast makes everyone forget.

I want to jump to my feet at the sight of my lovely bride, but I force myself to rise slowly. I take slow, measured steps down the dais and then extend my hand to her. She puts her small one in mine, her movements pretty and elegant, and when she smiles up at me, people cheer.

If nothing else, we have changed the mood at court, and that is something.

I tuck Halla's hand in my arm and nod at the chaperones that follow her. Penella and Ishera—two of my finest warriors—have been chosen to be my bride's chaperones. I chose them because they were female, and perhaps it is my own jealousy that makes me choose women for the roles. I want her to be comfortable, of course, and I know our ways are foreign to her.

More than that, though, I do not want another man looking upon what is mine. Yesterday was a necessity. I enjoyed looking at her lovely body, but it took everything I had not to cover her immediately. She is mine and mine alone, and my possessive streak grows greater with every moment that I am in her presence.

Princess Halla belongs to me.

If Halla is aware of my jealousy, she does not indicate it. She smiles and nods her head at the court as if this is any other feast and I am not about to take her to a private room and bury my face between her thighs. Some of the men have knowing looks on their faces, but I make sure that my glare lets them know that I will not have her embarrassed. I escort my bride to the doors of the great hall, and then we turn.

"Let the Tasting of the Bride begin!" I say in a ringing voice, and their cheers—of excitement and catcalls both—drown out our exit.

Then Halla and I are alone in the hall, Penella and Ishera silent shadows a span of steps behind us.

Halla does not look at me as we move through the halls. The sounds of merrymaking in the main hall carry through, echoing with our steps, and I wait until they die away before I turn to look at my bride. I have not seen her since last night, and I wondered if I would wake this morning and find her fled back to the temple.

"I am glad you have stayed," I lean in and murmur as we walk.

She gives me a startled look, two bright red flags of color in her cheeks. "You thought I would leave?"

I chuckle and pat the hand tucked into my arm. "I wasn't entirely sure after yesterday. But I thank you for honoring my people's customs. I know they're very different than yours, but if you are to be accepted as queen of the Cyclopae, a marriage following the old ways is wisest."

"Am I your queen, then?" Her voice is soft.

"Did you have any doubt?"

She makes a soft noise in her throat that I cannot decide is agreement or embarrassment. Halla gazes straight ahead, composing herself. "I was not certain of my place...in any of this."

I wonder how much more plainly I can tell her. I pause in my steps and turn to face her. The expression on her pretty face is practiced, as if she is afraid of showing any sort of emotion. "You are mine. I would not humiliate you with a pretend marriage. Nor do I have plans to abandon you. You are my wife, Halla...or you will be once this ceremony is over. That will make you Queen of Cyclopae, Adassia and Yshrem."

"And this is what you want, too?"

Frustrated, I grunt at her. "I'm not sure why you are so convinced that I do not know what I want."

"Because you could have a much younger wife—" she begins.

I groan. Not this again. I grab my regal bride by the waist—she is wearing Yshremi garb today, I see, the colors pale and milky and there are far too many layers—and heave her onto my shoulder, like the barbarian she thinks I am.

Halla squeaks in protest, her legs kicking once. "What are you doing?"

"I'm going to show you just how seriously I take this marriage." I turn to face Pen and Ishera. "What room has been set up for the ceremony?"

Ishera smirks at me and gestures ahead. "Down this hall. Double doors."

I stalk in the direction she points, hauling my bride with me. I have dreamed of this moment for years, and to see the hesitation on Halla's face stirs my temper...and a hint of worry. As a Cyclops bride, she can back out of our wedding at any time if she does not find me to be an amenable groom. I don't want to give her a chance to think about this and talk herself out of it.

The time to begin the ceremony is now. "Come, Halla."

"Do I have any choice?" she asks, but she doesn't sound irritated. Rather, she sounds amused, as if my arrogance and impatience is endearing to her. It's just another reason why I know we will be a good match.

I storm down the hall and make my way to the chamber that has been established for such a ceremony. In Cyclopae, our people live in tents and so a special tent is used for wedding rituals. We brought such a tent from our homelands, but I do not want Halla to feel even more out of place than she already does. I need her to feel comfortable, because what I am about to do to her is going to be very new. I don't want her getting skittish and crying off.

I don't know how much she knows of men, or if she knows anything at all. The thought is both incredibly appealing and intimidating. I've never tasted a woman's cunt, because I wanted to wait for her. I know from talking with other warriors that not every woman responds the same, and so I am prepared to lick and pleasure her for as long as it takes to ensure that she enjoys herself.

The pleasure, I think, will be mine as well. I've hungered to taste her.

I push into the room and the doors fly open, banging against the wall. Yshremi servant girls squeal in surprise and hurry out of the room, their heads bent. I glance around at the chamber. It is... well, it is ridiculous. Thick silks hang from the walls like banners of conquest, and flower petals of every color imaginable have been strewn about. In the corner, incense burns under a small altar to Magra, goddess of fertility. A large upraised platform in the center of the room has white furs piled upon it, and above the bed—because I suppose that must be a bed—is the banner that proclaims the unity of our two houses.

"Is...that a cheese tray?" Halla asks.

I turn to look. "Yes, it is." Along with wine and fruit. Gods above, do they think she's going to need a snack while I feast on her? Ishera giggles, and I turn to glare at the Cyclops warrior. She goes quiet, her lips twitching. I set my bride down gently, then shut the doors behind us.

The moment the doors are shut, Ishera and Penella move to opposite sides of the room and sit on low stools left there for them. They avert their eyes to give us the proper amount of privacy. Halla and I are alone, in a way. I know Penella and Ishera will say nothing of what transpires in this room. I have chosen them precisely for such a thing. I turn to Halla, who's fussing with her skirts and adjusting her clothing. She looks nervous. I gather her hands in mine. "Shall I tell you more about this portion of the ceremony?"

"I admit I'm curious," she tells me, and her face grows pink. "About the ritual of it, of course."

I grin. "Of course."

She opens her mouth to say something else, and then breaks off, flustered. "I thought yesterday might be the most challenging part of this marriage ceremony," Halla admits, her voice soft. "But I viewed that as a battle. This is...different."

I feel the same, in a sense. This is more intimate. Yesterday was a performance for her people and mine. Today is about her and me. I put my hands on her hips and steer her toward the fur bedding. "The story has it that the first cyclops king, Liandros, searched far and wide for a bride worthy of his line. He was known through many kingdoms as the finest warrior and none could best him in battle. He met many women, but none were able to withstand his fierce personality, and he wanted a bride that would challenge him."

"And did he find her?"

I caress Halla's cheek and love that she leans in to my touch. "He did. Right in his own tribe. One of his childhood friends, Siara, had become a warrior and given her eye to the god while Liandros was away on a journey. He returned and was smitten by her, but Siara would not have him. Instead, she demanded to know what he would bring to the marriage bed. He grew angry and ripped off her clothing in front of the entire tribe."

"He sounds awful." Her nose wrinkles daintily.

I laugh. "Liandros was not known for his patience. But he swore he would have Siara. She was angry at him after he shamed her, so he demanded to know what would change her mind. She told him if he could please her in bed with his hands tied behind his back, she would reconsider. He agreed and went to her bedchamber, and she refused to take his pants off for him. So Liandros was...creative. And his bride-to-be was very pleased." I caress her cheek. "So it is tradition for a Cyclops warrior to please his bride in bed before the final ceremony."

"I see. It is...very different than Yshremi weddings." She does not meet my eyes.

I can imagine that it is. The Yshremi are a scholarly people who love farming and books. I imagine most of my people's customs are very foreign to them. "Then I feel sorry for Yshremi women."

Halla looks up and gives me a shocked glance.

"Shall you bind my hands behind my back?" I state boldly, crossing my wrists in front of her. "Or will you allow me to touch you on this evening?"

"I...what exactly is involved?" My sweet bride looks utterly flustered. "I don't...I mean..." She wrings her hands. "When I was prepared for the marriage bed, I was told about treaties and king-

doms and how not to cede my power to my husband in an argument. Not much was said about the marriage bed itself other
than I should be patient with my husband's attentions and not
interrupt."

Not interrupt? What a strange thing to teach a woman. But then
again, the Yshremi treat their daughters very different than
Cyclopae do. "You can interrupt me as much as you want if I do
something you don't like."

"Very well." Halla looks gravely earnest.

I caress her cheek and then gesture at the bed. "Let us sit down,
then." When she nods, I guide her over to the edge of the bed and
sit, and she sits across from me. I'd hoped she would sit in my lap,
but I can be patient. She's clearly rattled.

I caress her cheek as she watches me. Her gaze flicks to Pen and
Ishera. "Those are the chaperones? They're staying, then?" Her
voice is hushed, as if she doesn't want them to overhear her.

I nod. "It's to ensure you aren't pressured or uncomfortable
should you change your mind halfway through. Some of our
warriors have been known to be overly enthusiastic in the past
and ended up with a knife in their gut." I shrug. "I think they just
did not use their tongues correctly—"

Her hand claps over my mouth, her expression scandalized. "We
shouldn't talk about such things."

We shouldn't? Perhaps she'd just rather I show her, instead. I
move her hand from my mouth. "Shall I start with a kiss?" I press
my lips against her palm. After all, nothing says I cannot start
with kisses before I move between her thighs. It's all about giving
her pleasure, and I know she likes kissing.

Halla's expression goes soft, her gaze on my mouth as I nibble at
her tender skin. Her hands are soft, but there are hints of fading

calluses that remind me that she lived a meager life in Riekki's temple for the last sixteen years, and I am filled with frustration. She has always tried to do the right thing, Halla. I remember that fateful day well. Instead of letting others murder me, even after she heard of her father's death at my father's hands, she protected me, cared for me. She made sure I was safe and returned to my father unharmed. She ordered her Yshremi warriors to stand down, because she did not want anyone else to die. And she gave up her crown so she would save lives. It seems unfair that she should then be punished with sixteen years of solitude. I know Riekki's peacekeepers. They are a pious order that loves nothing more than hard work and silence.

I think of the poetry book, hidden under the guise of a book of prayers, and cannot help but grin to myself. Even in such a holy place, she dreamed of something more. I plan on giving it to her. "I have always loved you," I tell her as I push her sleeve up and kiss her wrist. "Ever since I was a small boy, I told everyone who would listen that I would marry Princess Halla of Yshrem. That there was no one as beautiful and kind as her. No one as glorious." With each word, I press my mouth against her skin, traveling up her arm.

"I wonder how your father felt about such devotion," she says, and her voice is breathless and sweet, her gaze fixed on my mouth so intently.

"He disagreed," I say, and lean in to kiss the crook of her elbow. "But he is dead and I am now king, and I do what I want."

She shivers, and I don't know if it's from my mouth or my words. It doesn't matter. Nothing will change my mind. Halla is and always will be mine from this point forward.

When I can press her sleeve no higher, I nibble my way back down her arm and then give her hand one final kiss. I gaze up at her and she watches me with heavy-lidded eyes, her lips parted. She looks so ready for my cock that there is a deep, intense ache in my groin.

I slide an arm around her waist and pull her close, until her breasts are pressed up against my chest. Her eyes widen, but she doesn't protest. Instead, her hand slides up to my nape and she touches my hair, curling her fingers in it.

And waits. She's so beautiful as she looks up at me with breathless anticipation.

I lower my mouth to hers, and her lips part under mine. The kiss is just as good this time as I remembered, and I stroke my tongue into the sweet heat of her mouth. I love the little moan that escapes her, and the way she clings to me as I deepen the kiss, using my tongue as I want to use my cock, claiming her with every possessive stroke. Our lips meld over and over, until I forget all about who else is in the room. There's no one that exists outside of the gorgeous princess in my arms. She shifts against me and I hitch her closer, until she's practically in my lap, and her thigh is pressing up against my cock in an almost-painful reminder of just how very hard she makes me. Panting, I release her mouth from mine with a last reluctant nip, because I could spend all night kissing her, lost in her lips.

Halla's fingers tighten in my hair and then she presses her mouth shyly to mine. "There's nothing that says I cannot kiss you back, is there?"

I bite back my groan. "Nothing at all."

And then the lovely creature takes control of our embrace and begins to kiss me all on her own. Her kisses are small, soft, nipping ones that tease rather than conquer. I am fascinated by this, because I know it's purely instinctual. This is how Halla works, I realize—with small nibbles and little caresses, unlike my brutal conquest of her mouth. It is another reason we will be good together as rulers.

Of course, my cock could be making me think of all kinds of assumptions, but I don't care. In this moment she could hold me down and ravage my mouth and I would think she was the loveliest, most delicate creature ever. She could do anything to me and I would willingly submit.

My princess makes a little noise in her throat as she kisses me, her arms twining around my neck, and I realize she wants me to kiss her back. Her playful nips stop once I kiss her back, and then we are using our tongues to dance along each other's mouths in a sensual alternation of licks that make me imagine her mouth everywhere.

I kiss her softly one more time and then pull away. "Let me lay you back on the bed, love."

Wariness flares in her eyes, and she gives me a nervous nod. She sits back on the bed and then smooths her skirts down her legs. "What now?"

I see the tips of her slippers peeping out from underneath her skirts. I take one foot in my hand and casually pull the shoe off, tossing it aside. Her eyes go wide and she gazes at me, frozen in place. I can feel her quiver as I caress her ankle, and I remove the other shoe and then just rub her feet for a moment, trying to get her to relax. If anything, my touch only makes her more nervous.

"Tell me about your time in the temple," I murmur. I'm trying to distract her, and I hope it works.

"The temple?" she echoes, a confused look on her face. Her gaze flicks back and forth between my hands and my face.

"Yes. Did you enjoy your time there?"

Halla looks at me as if I am growing a second head. "Did I enjoy living as a fugitive? Wondering if this is the day that assassins will arrive to kill me and resolve all claim to the throne? Being looked at as an outsider by the peacekeepers because I was not one of them, and them unable to do anything about me because of who I am?"

I should not have asked. "I hate that you went through that."

She softens at my words and shrugs her shoulders. "It was not what I had anticipated my path to be." Her voice is low, sad. "I had been trained since a young age that I would make a marriage to strengthen Yshrem. I admit I didn't know what to do with myself for a very long time when I arrived at the temple. No one wants a spinster once-queen who gave her throne to the barbarians."

"You did what you had to do to save lives. Surely you see that?" I've stopped rubbing her feet, because this is going in a direction I don't want. Instead of relaxing her and distracting her, she's growing sad.

"Not everyone understands a decision a ruler makes." Her smile is small. "I should not complain. You saved my life sixteen years ago when you told your father I protected you. You made it sound like I stood before the sword like the bravest of warriors."

"Were you not? You faced your men as calmly as any queen."

"But I was queen."

"Aye, and it would have been very easy for them to cut your throat, blame my father's men, and then take the throne for themselves. Instead, you stood up for the enemy because you felt it was the right thing to do."

"I would never let someone kill a child simply because he had the wrong father."

"Neither would I." I grin and slide to my knees, and then I am kneeling on the floor in front of her feet. "See? We are agreed. You saved my life, and I saved yours. We are equals."

"Mmm." She doesn't sound as if she agrees with me. That's all right. She doesn't have to agree. Now, I am in a position of power. I am king and I do and take what I want.

And right now, I cannot wait to take my bride.

I lift her foot carefully and kiss the arch.

She gasps, shaken by my touch. Her eyes go soft and she watches me intently.

"Ticklish?" I ask, loving how responsive she is. She can't hide how she feels, and I love that her normal dignified manner has disappeared and there's a skittish, fascinated woman with me instead of the aloof, regal princess. She's both, and I love both sides of her, but there's only one I want in my bed.

"I don't know," Halla admits. "No one's ever touched my feet like that before."

"How does it make you feel, then?" I lean in and kiss the arch again, letting my tongue brush against the underside as I pull away.

She sucks in a breath and squirms on the bed, her gaze locked onto me. "I...I don't know." She's breathless. "This is all very...new."

My bride is very untouched. I can't help the fierce surge of pleasure I feel at that. "Tell me if you don't like something that I do, then."

Halla nods and remains still as I kiss her foot again, then move up to her ankle. She's silent as I continue to kiss my way forward, pressing my mouth against the soft skin of her ankle and calf. I love her delicate bones and how I can feel every tremor that moves through her. She doesn't pull away, though, and when I pause, a flicker of disappointment crosses her face until I lean in once more.

Perhaps I'm going too slow to please my bride. I want to take my time to ensure that she is comfortable, but perhaps I should push things further. I slide a hand up her graceful calf and push her skirts back until her legs are revealed all the way up to the knee. She says nothing, but the pink flush brightens on her cheeks. She reaches down and gathers the skirts in her hands...and then slowly pulls them higher, revealing white thighs and a tantalizing glimpse of pantaloons that ruffle just below her hips.

It feels like an invitation. And when she bites her lip and gives me an anxious look, I know it is one.

I press forward and graze my mouth over her ankle again, then begin to work my way slowly upward, just as I did with her arm. She's trembling, but the soft rasp of her breath tells me that it's excitement more than fear. I kiss her calf, then her knee, and then move up to the creamy flesh of her thigh. At this point, she gives a little whimper in her throat, and shifts on the bedding.

I kiss higher, caressing her hands before I push her skirts even further up her thighs. Her pantaloons are fully revealed to me and she squirms under my gaze, restless as I stare down at her. "You're beautiful," I murmur, keeping my voice low so it feels as if we are the only two in the room. I know Pen and Ishera will be as quiet as possible, but I want Halla to forget that they're there. I want her to focus on me and only me. "May I take these off?"

And I lean in and bite the ruffle gracing the edge of one pantaloon leg.

Halla's lips part, and she gives a shuddering breath. "I...should I get undressed all the way?"

"Do you want to?"

She hesitates. "I don't know." Her gaze flicks to the women at the edge of the room.

"I can pleasure you under your skirts, too, you know." I give her my cockiest grin, as if my own heart is not pounding as loud as a blacksmith's hammer. "No one will see your beauty but me. Perhaps we'll save the rest for tomorrow night, yes?"

She flushes prettily and bites her lip, then nods.

I smile at her, because she's beyond beautiful, and then slide my hands up her thighs, all the way to the waistband of her pantaloons. Slowly, I edge them downward, revealing more pale skin and a gently rounded belly. The way she looked yesterday in the throne room has been burned into my mind, and I'm eager to see her naked once more. More than that, I'm eager to taste her. I've longed to put my mouth on her cunt for ages. I've dreamed of marrying her in the custom of my people, and in my dreams, she reacts with pleasure and is hungry for more. Thus far, the real Halla has surpassed every one of my dreams.

I cannot wait to see how this plays out in comparison.

I gently slide the fabric all the way down to her thighs, and the peep of the curls between her thighs is fully exposed to my gaze. Even here, she is delicate and feminine, and I cannot resist moving forward and pressing my mouth there in a kiss.

The breath rushes out of her, half gasp, half moan. One hand clenches against my shoulder and then falls away.

"You can touch me," I tell her, grasping her hand and pulling it back against my skin. "Touch me all you want. I like it."

"Mathior," Halla whispers, and she caresses my jaw. Her eyes are soft. "Sometimes this feels as if I'm dreaming. Am I dreaming?"

"Let me show you how real this is," I say, and then I rip her pantaloons away. I don't care that I'm destroying delicate, embroidered fabric. I want her naked and under my tongue right now. I've hungered for this for far too long. I push her thighs apart and then my mouth is on her.

She cries out, her hands going to my head. A second later, she twists her fingers in my hair and her hips buck up against my face. I grip one of her hips to hold her as she writhes, and keep my mouth on her flesh. The seam of her cunt is incredibly wet, and I drag my tongue over it, determined to take my time and learn her.

And with that lick, I get my first taste of my woman. It's musky and intense and my mouth waters, hungry for more. She's perfect, even here, and I give her another deep lick, pushing apart her folds with my tongue and burrowing deeper into her sweetness. I learn her with the tip of my tongue, tracing the layers of her cunt and learning which touches she likes. When I come to the nub of her clit, the breath explodes from her body. "Mathior!"

"I have you," I tell her between urgent licks. I don't want to let her go. Being here, my face cradled by her thighs as I nuzzle and lick the most intimate part of her? I could stay here forever, lapping at her cunt and enjoying every tremor that rocks through her body. "Let me taste you, Halla. Let me taste all of you."

She whimpers, and her hips quiver in my grip. Her hands tighten in my hair, but I ignore it, because when I lick her clit, her body gives a little jerk and she gasps. I want more of those little gasps. So I circle her clit with my tongue, then lick it directly. Halla arches up against me, and so I do it again, and again. She's responding, but I have not yet made her come.

And I want to make her come, very much. I will not be worthy of being her husband if I do not give her pleasure.

I flick my tongue against the underside of her clit, then experiment with the pace of my licking, watching her responses. She shudders when I suck and press directly against her clit, but she makes sweet sounds of pleasure when I rub near it, but not quite touch. Fascinating. I focus in on rubbing around her clit instead of on it directly, and when she moans, I grip her thighs a little tighter, my own excitement spurring me on. It takes everything I have not to grab her and frantically lick her to a climax, because she's not like me. The quicker and rougher I touch her won't make her come faster. So I continue to give her the teasing touches that she needs, my tongue dancing and flirting along the hood of her clit and never quite touching it.

I love when she starts to pant, her body wriggling against me. "Mathior," she gasps, and the hand in my hair tightens. "I don't...wait...I don't know..."

"Tell me to stop and I will," I murmur briefly and then lower my head again, devoting more of my attention to her. I want to take her to the next level, to make her wild, and so I slide one hand under my mouth and begin to pet her cunt in the places that I cannot yet devote my tongue to. I stroke a finger against the entrance to her core and when she tightens, I tease the tip of it in even as I continue to lap at her clit.

"No," she pants, arching up underneath me as if she can press herself against my mouth. "No...don't stop. Please. Mathior!" Her voice grows more urgent and full of need with every stroke of my tongue.

My cock strains against my leathers and I force myself not to rub back and forth against the edge of the bed, lest I come and not finish pleasuring my woman first. I need her to come, and come hard and so good that she aches to marry me. An unsatisfied female can turn away the man that asks for her hand in marriage, and I aim not to be that man.

I push a finger into her cunt and nearly lose control at how tight and wet she is. Halla moans in pleasure, and I feel a new rush of her honey against my tongue. She's close, if the flex and quiver of her cunt is any indication. Her gasps and cries increase with frequency and she rocks her hips wildly against my mouth. Her excitement is spurring mine, and it's taking everything I have not to spill into my leather breeches. I thrust into her with my finger, pumping into her cunt as I want to with my cock. It's not part of the "tasting," but I can't help myself. I'm too addicted to the soft cries she makes and the sensation of her body clenching around my finger. I push another one in alongside the first, and then I'm slowly fucking her with my fingers as I lap at her cunt.

Her thighs quiver and she gives a guttural cry. Her cunt spasms around my fingers and then her honey floods my mouth. She arches up against my mouth as she climaxes, and I keep on nuzzling her, determined to wring out her climax for as long as possible. With a whimper, she shudders and then goes limp on the furs, as if she's lost all the strength in her body.

I continue to lap at her cunt, unwilling to let this moment end. I feel fierce satisfaction that I've made her climax so hard. Halla trembles with every stroke of my tongue, and I keep going until her thighs start to slide together and it's clear she doesn't want me there any longer. I still want to do more, of course. My body throbs with awareness of her, and her scent is in my nose, her taste on my tongue. How do other bridegrooms possibly stop when their woman is sprawled in bed in front of them, bare to the waist? I give the inside of her thigh a fervent kiss. "My Halla."

She makes a breathless sound that might be a response.

I move forward on the bed, crawling over her. My pants are still on and I won't do anything—not tonight—but I want to hold her, see her face as she recovers from her climax. I move next to her on the bed and caress her cheek, rubbing my nose against her skin. I want to kiss her, but I also don't want to lose the taste of her cunt on my lips. "My sweet love."

Halla's eyes are glazed, her lips pink and plump from biting them. Her hair is disheveled and there's a faint sheen of sweat on her face. I've never seen her look more beautiful.

She moans and puts a hand to my face, kissing me ferociously.

I pull her into my arms, slicking my tongue into her mouth, giving her all the urgency I feel. We share hungry kisses and then she pulls away, panting. "That was...I...there are no words."

"Did I please you?" I rub my nose against hers. I want to stay here forever, I think, and just drink in...her.

"Oh yes," she tells me, breathless. Her hand skims up and down my chest, as if she cannot stop touching me, either. "But you..."

"Tomorrow." I close my eyes and press a kiss to her hand. My need for her nearly overwhelms me and I hold her hand to my mouth, breathing deep.

"Did you get no pleasure tonight, then?"

"My pleasure was entirely in pleasing you, my love."

She pulls her hand from my grip and slides it down my chest, then moves to the waist of my pants. "Can I...touch you? The way you touched me?" And she boldly cups my cock.

The breath leaves my body. "You want to touch me?"

"Is it allowed?" She hesitates, starts to pull her hand from my groin.

I push it back there, because I want her touch more than I want air. "Anything you wish," I tell her.

Halla's lips part and then she caresses my cock with a bold stroke. I close my eyes, because her touch is making me desperately close to losing control.

"You're bigger than I imagined," she whispers, all the while her fingers tracing and outlining my length, learning it with a touch. "Are you sensitive here?" When I nod, she gives me a fascinated look, continuing to stroke me through my pants. "What feels good? How should I touch you? You knew how to caress me, and this is all new." She leans in close to me, her lips near enough to brush over mine and whispers. "And I want to learn."

With a groan, I grip her hand and show her just how to touch me. I don't use the same gentle touches she does. Mine are brutal and swift, and the sight of her lips parting in wonder as I use her hand to rub myself to climax is the most beautiful thing I've ever seen. Her name is on my tongue as I come, swift and hard. I spill into my leather breeches with an almost-painful joy and then fall back onto the blankets, utterly spent.

Halla caresses my face, fascinated. "That was pleasing?"

I huff out a laugh. "Pleasing" seems too simple a word, too benign. "Completely."

She burrows into the blankets against my side and rests her cheek on my shoulder. "What now?"

I pull her close and stroke her hair, caressing her everywhere I can. I'm not ready to give her up yet, though I know I must. One more day, I remind myself. One more day and she's truly mine. "Now you must tell the witnesses if I pleased you or not, and then we must be separated until the ceremony."

"Oh." Halla frowns and presses her face against my shoulder. "I'm not sure I'm ready to leave yet."

I love that she says that. "It is only one day more and you will be secluded until the wedding, as will I. This is to allow either of us the opportunity to refuse the marriage at any time up until we are brought before the priests."

"Ah. And if I decided to refuse to marry you?"

Even thinking of such a thing pains me, but I promised I'd give her a choice. "I would tell everyone that you met an unfortunate death the evening before our wedding and would have you taken to the temple of your choice. If the peacekeepers do not suit you, we will find you another home." I stroke the hair back from her lovely face. "I meant what I said when I told you that you would always be safe with me."

A frown mars Halla's face. "But if I am supposedly killed the evening before our wedding, won't people assume you have done something terrible to me?"

"Let them assume what they like. It doesn't matter."

"It matters to me! The Yshremi people don't trust you as it is. If you hope for any sort of peace..."

If I do not have Halla, all of Yshrem can burn for all I care. I do not say such a thing, though, because I do not want her to feel obligated. I want her to come to me because she wants me. Because she enjoyed my mouth on her cunt. Because she wants more kisses and caresses.

Because she wants me.

I know that what I ask might be impossible. That her feelings toward me will always be colored by her father's death and the conquest of her kingdom by my father. But I have always seen her as Halla, the lovely girl who saved me when I was a child. I want her to see me as more than just King of Cyclopae.

So we will see.

I sit up and help her straighten her clothing. I want to lie in this bed with her for hours on end, but I know that will not be wise. I am king, but even a king must bow to custom every now and then. I help her to her feet and then cup her cheek one last time. "I will see you tomorrow, my love."

"You keep calling me that," Halla murmurs.

"So I do." I don't explain myself. Let her determine what she will. I know how I feel.

She gives me a tremulous smile and then smooths her hands over her hair. As she does, the regal, distant expression moves over her face once more and Princess Halla is back, shy virgin Halla retreating inside her. She gathers her skirts and heads for the door to the room. Ishera and Pen flank her on the way out. They will get her answer privately and then reveal it in the court before those who have arrived for the feast. Not many grooms are humiliated by their future brides before those gathered before the wedding—and that is because every cyclops warrior does his best to ensure that his woman is well pleasured before he leaves her.

I do not think Halla's answer will be a poor one. However, that doesn't mean she won't change her mind before the wedding. For a moment, I hesitate, wondering if there was more I could have done. If I should have pleasured her longer, made her come three or four or ten times. If that would change her mind, if it can even be changed at this point.

But no amount of licking and pleasuring will change Halla's mind if she decides she cannot marry a cyclops.

10

HALLA

I'm still numb with shock as the two female Cyclopae return me to my rooms. They didn't smirk when I gave them my answer—that yes, Mathior pleased me in bed. I like them immensely for that. Then I'm sent back to my chambers and I'm alone. I sit down on the edge of the bed and stare out at my room, dazed.

Even though this is the same room I left just a short while ago, I feel like a different person. The blankets and bedding are fine Yshremi weave, but I pick up the fur-trimmed cloak at the foot of my bed and touch the soft edging, because the white of it reminds me of Mathior's cloak. I gaze up at the banner on the wall. Once upon a time, my father's family crest hung there, and a tapestry of Yshremi legends covered the other wall. Those are gone, and in their place, the banns hang as if reminding me that the ruling house of Yshrem will be united with the Cyclopae king tomorrow.

As if I could possibly forget.

I squeeze my thighs together and tremble. I'm still damp and throbbing from where he touched me. If I close my eyes and think hard enough, I can almost feel his tongue there, exploring my folds and doing things I've never dreamed of. It was just like in the book, and it felt better than I ever imagined. My nipples tighten at the memory and I resist the urge to run my hand over them. If this "tasting" was so good, I cannot possibly imagine how wondrous the marriage bed will be.

I'm actually...excited about the prospect. I can't stop blushing, either. Mathior doesn't seem to care that I'm eight years older than him and probably past my best childbearing years. All he cares about is...me. Kissing me. Talking to me. Tasting me. He calls me his love. I'm utterly dazzled by him. I know I should be thinking strategically about how I can use the throne to push for Yshrem, to ensure that they are not completely overrun by Cyclopae wars and customs, but all I can think of is Mathior. His smile. His kiss.

His tongue.

Gods above, but I am utterly infatuated with him. I fling myself back on my bed and sigh like the young girl I no longer am.

"Whore," someone spits at me.

I sit upright on my bed, glancing around my room. I thought I was alone. Fear hammers through me and I go stiff as an elderly woman emerges from my private garderobe and into my chambers. She doesn't carry a knife, but that doesn't mean she isn't here to do me harm. "Who are you?" My voice is calm and steady. "What are you doing in my rooms?"

"I am one of your people." She scowls at me as if I am dirt beneath her feet, her lip curling in disdain. She pushes into my room as if she owns it, storming toward me to point one age-withered finger in my face. "And you should be ashamed!"

I'm too stunned to say anything. There are guards outside my chambers. I could scream and they would be on this woman in an instant. She'd be sent to the dungeons—or simply executed for putting my life in danger. And yet...she carries no knife on her, no rope to strangle me—if she even could with her wizened arms. And she is Yshremi, as I am. "Ashamed?"

"For spreading your thighs for that cyclops! He and his people murdered your father! Stole our lands!" Her eyes shimmer with tears. "Destroyed everything our people stood for. My sons died in that war. Sixteen years and we've hated the cyclops invaders with every beat of our hearts. Imagine how it felt to hear that Princess Halla, last of the royal line of Yshrem, would be marrying the beast that killed her father."

"Mathior didn't—" I whisper, but she cuts me off with a baleful glare.

"He's the spawn of King Alistair, is he not? You might as well coat your bed in your father's blood."

I flinch, because her words are cruel. "It's not like that."

"Is it not? Do you think he wants you because you are young and nubile?" She gives me another scornful look. "Because you are rich? Or simply because it's an easy way for him to quell any sort of uprisings? And you are foolish enough to fall for such a thing!"

Her words are like daggers. I lean away from her as she looms over me, and I feel like a naughty child. "It's not like that," I say weakly. "He loves me. He told me."

"Of course he said that. You would have to be a monumental fool to marry him if he treated you as if he hated you." She lifts her chin and gives me another scowl. "I hope his mouth is worth the lives of your people."

I'm shocked at the vitriol in her voice. I simply stare at her, aghast, until she crosses her arms over her chest. "Are you going to call the guards on me? Have me executed for telling you the truth?"

My mouth works silently for a moment. "No," I say finally. How can I when she's one of my people? She doesn't understand how it is between myself and Mathior. How kind and caring he is. How much he loves me and makes me feel pretty.

You would have to be a monumental fool to marry him if he treated you as if he hated you.

Am I a fool? As I remain on the bed, silent, she harrumphs and returns to my garderobe and shuts the door behind her once more. I hear something that sounds like the scrape of stone. A secret passage, then. Castle Yshrem is filled with them. I get to my feet and lock the door, then press on the side of the large wooden trunk against the wall until it's in front of the door.

I return to my bed, my happiness draining out of me instantly.

Am I falling for pretty words and a talented tongue simply because it's an easy way to subdue the budding Yshremi uprising? Is Mathior truly that devious?

Can I marry him? Should I? I pick up the cloak with the white fur edging and pet it, but it no longer gives me pleasure. All I can think of is Mathior and his smile...and I wonder if I am betraying my people.

I have a day to decide.

11

The Next Day

MATHIOR

The wedding ceremony will be held in the Hour of Storms, at sunset. That is the hour devoted to the god of battle and patron of the Cyclops, Aron of the Cleaver. I spend the afternoon in prayer, offering up gifts and the promises of many future battles if only I get what I want this day.

And what I want is Halla.

But Aron, if he is listening, has always known this. My prayers have not changed in sixteen years: I want a long life full of glory and battle, prosperity for my people, and Halla at my side. I never make demands of the gods, but on this day, I send a fervent thank you to Aron of the Cleaver for granting me at least some of that. Hours from now, Halla will be mine. I will kiss her lovely face, take her to my bed, and make her my wife. No one will take her from me ever again, and she will be at my side, always. I do not care if we live in Cyclopae in tents, or if she wishes we settle in Yshrem. There are initial visits to be made to my other lands, of course, but after that I do not care where we go. Let her choose. I will be content as long as she is in my bed.

The strongest offerings are those of blood, though, and I pull out my knife, say a prayer to Aron once more, and then cut a deep slice into the meat of my bicep. Not my sword arm, because only fools would do such a thing. Aron wants no fools worshiping him, I imagine. I set down the knife on the altar and raise the prayer bowl to my arm, watching it fill with blood. When it is done, I bind the wound and leave the room to dress for my wedding.

Soon, I tell myself. Halla will be yours soon.

I return to my chambers and the advisors flutter around, trying to give me advice as I dress. I put on my leatherwork leggings that are decorated with beaded tassels down the legs, one for each kill I've made in battle. I shave the side of my head, and then my jaw as the advisors prattle on about treaties and borders. I let them talk themselves into circles without interrupting, since I figured out long ago that it was arguing for the sake of arguing more than needing advice. I rub a hand over my jaw to make sure there's no stubble, thinking of Halla's soft thighs and how sensitive they were. I don't want to scrape her skin.

Two advisors argue over the printing of coins in Yshrem and whether or not they should have my profile or a symbol. That is easy to answer—one side shall have my Halla's face, and the other will have mine.

"I do not like that you give her so much power, First Warrior," one of the advisors begins.

"Then it is a good thing I did not ask you," I tell him easily and find a mirror on the wall. It is tradition for a father to paint his

son with the Cyclopae symbols before his marriage, but my
father is dead and I am surrounded by fools who try to tell me
not to marry my woman. I will simply do it myself. I paint Aron's
cleaver over my breast in bright red, and then remove my
eyepatch, regarding my face in the mirror. When Halla knew me,
I had two eyes. Does she find this ugly, I wonder. Or does she
understand that tradition goes deep with my people? The eye-
scar has always been seen as one of pride and honor amongst my
people.

But...I want Halla to enjoy looking at me, as I enjoy looking
at her.

Bah. I am being a nervous fool. Irritated at myself for worrying
over such things, I smear a dark red line of paint down my scar,
from brow to cheekbone, mimicking Aron scarring from his
battle with the Great Dragon One-Tooth. I paint the symbols of
my father's line down my arms and across my stomach, and then
sit cross-legged on the floor and do my best to meditate while I
wait. Once the ceremonial paint is dry, I will put on my white fur
cloak and descend to the throne room, where my bride will be
presented to me.

"First Warrior," one particularly noxious advisor says, a hint of
whine in his voice.

"What?" I do not open my eye or shift in my repose. "I am busy."

"There is a, ah, problem, First Warrior."

I bite back the impatience I feel. "Can it wait until after my
wedding?"

There's a long hesitation that fills me with uneasiness. "It's about
the wedding," the advisor says eventually. "I'm not sure there will
be one."

I open my eye and glare at him. "Speak freely and tell me what you mean."

The man swallows hard and gives his fellow advisors an uncertain look. After a moment, he steps forward and clears his throat. "I have, ah, been notified that it is past time for your bride to participate in the ceremonial bathing and she has not arrived. Nor will she answer when anyone knocks at her door. She will not open for anyone."

I get to my feet slowly, my heart thudding in my chest. "She has refused me, then?" The world has turned to gray ash in an instant. "She will not become my queen?"

A drop of nervous sweat rolls down the man's nose and splashes onto the front of his robe. "We-we-we don't know, First Warrior," he stammers. "Princess Halla does not answer at all."

I storm out of my chambers. "Take me to her at once."

12

HALLA

I stare out the window of my room, down at the courtyard below, and think about sixteen years that have passed. Sixteen years ago, I was young and arrogant and thought nothing in the world could change for me. I knew my father had gone to war with the Cyclopae, but I lived inside a sheltered cocoon and thought it would truly not affect us. Even when the cyclops warriors camped outside our walls, I did not think it would end badly. Up until the very end, I knew with certainty that my father would win.

And then they brought me news of his death and everything changed.

I am not that same Halla, but I wonder if perhaps I have still been too cocooned. That I have been so sheltered from the world— first by court, and then by the peacekeepers of Riekki—that I cannot see a lie when it is in front of my face.

I am terrified of making the wrong decision, because this is final. Once I choose, I cannot un-crack that egg, as the saying goes. I will be Mathior's Yshremi bride, and I will either be the betrayer of my kingdom or a beloved bride.

I do not trust my own judgment to determine which one I will be. Ever since Mathior returned to my life, I have been completely besotted with him as any young woman would be. I am thirty-three and yet I find myself giggling over the thought of him when I am alone. He haunts my dreams. He is the first thing on my mind when I open my eyes and the last thing when I go to bed at night. When I touch myself in my bath, I think of him and his hot eyes and the confidence in his grin.

Sixteen years and I am not any wiser than that foolish princess who held a crown for an hour. I could not see my future then, and I cannot see it now.

I still have time to back out of this marriage, if it is the wrong thing to do. I am too taken by Mathior to think clearly. I don't know if he is playing me for a fool or if he truly cares for me. Because oh, I want him. I want him so badly I ache with it, and I worry I will destroy what is left of my kingdom if I pursue my heart.

What if those bewitching grins are lies? What if when he calls me "love" he's simply saying it because it dazzles me and because it's what I wish to hear? That I am so desperate and needy for affection that I can run to the arms of my enemy and not think about what it means?

I want him. I want him so badly I ache with it—not just between my thighs but deep in my soul. But this is the first decision I've had to make in sixteen years and I worry I'll make the wrong one just because I'm a lonely spinster who's seeing all of her dreams come true.

Mathior could be a great pretender. This could all be a game for him, some sort of devious ploy to grind Yshrem under his thumb once more, and I'm walking into it with a gleeful heart. I'm trying to be objective, but I don't know if I can.

Because all I can think about is Mathior's smile, his mouth between my thighs and the sounds of pleasure he made as he touched me, the fall of his hair over my legs, and the way he looked at me when I caressed him. The way he makes me feel like I'm the only thing that matters.

I press my hands to my face, fighting back the scream that wants to erupt.

I don't know what to do. Please, Father, help me. I want Mathior, but I don't know if it's wrong. Give me a sign. I open my eyes and gaze out the window, but the only sight that greets me is the sight of the Cyclopae tents on the far side of the wall and the banner of our joined house symbols. Am I supposed to read something from that? Or am I seeing answers where there are none? With a frustrated sigh, I turn away.

There's an urgent knock at my door.

I ignore it, as I have ignored all of them thus far. I know it's the ladies assigned to wait on me. They need to bathe me and dress me for the wedding, and I have no answer yet. If I am cautious and wary, I will back out of this marriage until I know for sure if Mathior speaks truly. My fear is that if I back out, I humiliate him and make matters worse instead of better. That he will change his mind and not want to marry me at all, and then I will return to Riekki's temple, broken-hearted and filled with regret.

The knock comes again, and then a third time. Muffled male voices call on the other side, but I move back to the window and lean over the edge, drinking in the fresh air. This was the view I had sixteen years ago, but it was a different wall around the keep itself, and back then it was spring and the air was not crisp with fall. Back then, I waited in this room with my ladies as the world wrecked itself below. I sat and sewed while my father died on a battlefield and took half his army with him and all the hopes of Yshrem. Saddest of all, I can't even remember why my father fought with Cyclopae and its king. Was it over a land dispute? Unlikely, because the Cyclopae borders are ever-changing and their people mostly nomadic. Their cities are tent cities, not stone like ours. Over a woman? Also unlikely—my father was ever-devoted to my mother's memory, and she died in childbirth. I suspect it was a war fought over egos, arrogance and perceived insults.

Such a shame.

The pounding at the door is more insistent, and then stops entirely. Good. Maybe they'll leave me in peace for a time and I can concentrate. I rub a hand at my temples, thinking.

In the next moment, there's a heavy thunk in the door that makes me jump. I turn, frowning, and it thunks again. Again. Again. Quick and relentless, it doesn't sound like knocking at all, but the brittle sound that wood makes when an axe hits it...

A moment later, the next slam is even louder, and an axe head pokes through the wood. I stare, wide-eyed and in shock as a hole gapes in the heavy slats of my door. The hole is widened with a few more chops, and then a familiar face peers through the hole. It's Mathior, his scar covered with bright red paint. He gazes inside, and then his mouth thins at the sight of me. With a muffled curse, he slams his fist through the hole, enlarging it until he can reach an arm through, and then pulls the heavy bar off my door and flips the latch. A moment later, he storms into my room.

I back up against the cool stone of the wall, my heart racing. His face is hard with an unreadable expression, and my throat goes dry. Is he angry that I'm stalling? Has he come to tell me that he's changed his mind? The thought stabs me with pain, but I lift my chin and don't move from my spot near the window.

Mathior comes to my side, and as he does, I see he's covered in even more paint, red symbols on his chest and arms. He pulls me against him, his gaze roaming over my body and then resting on my face. "Are you unwell? Hurt?" He puts a hand to my brow. "Fevered?"

"No," I say, startled by his intensity. I feel a little foolish because I have been worrying like mad, and yet this is not the expression of a man who cares nothing for his bride. This is a man worried for my well-being, and love and happiness bloom in my breast.

He takes in my words and then notices the wide-open shutters of the large window in my room, and how close I'm standing to it. A look of pure agony flickers across his face, then disappears.

I realize he thinks I meant to kill myself and I shake my head quickly. "Not that. I was just...thinking."

"Thinking," he echoes. "Of what?"

I try to smile. "My father, oddly enough."

It only makes his expression more intense. His hands grip my shoulders tightly, and then someone clears a throat behind us.

"Leave us," Mathior says, and his voice is flat and devoid of emotion.

A robed, bearded man steps forward. "But First Warrior, it is against custom to leave a groom alone with his bride before the weddi—"

Mathior turns and gives the man such a fierce look that the interloper visibly flinches. He bows and hurries back out, ushering the others along with him. A second later, the door is shut and I am alone in the room with my soon-to-be husband. He turns back to me and his mouth thins into a line.

"Are you this unhappy, Halla? I would not force you into marriage."

"You're not forcing me," I say quickly. "I simply had to think for a while and clear my head. Make sure that this was the right thing to do."

He leans in, searching my face as if looking for lies. "I did not please you last night?"

My face flames hot immediately. "That wasn't it."

"So you were pleased?"

Gods, he's really going to make me answer that. I give a jerky nod, mortified, and before I can say more, he sags to his knees before me, arms wrapped around my waist as he holds me close. "Halla," he murmurs, voice husky. "I have aged a hundred years in the last handful of minutes."

I want to stroke the glossy black head that is so close, and I hesitate...then decide that he's going to be mine, is he not? I can touch him. So I put a hand on his head and caress him, sliding my fingers through his thick hair. "I'm sorry if I worried you. I needed time to think and make sure that I was making the right decision and not being led astray by my heart."

His head presses against my belly and he takes in a deep breath. "Someone spoke to you. Made you doubt me."

"Mmm," I say noncommittally, because I don't want the old woman to die. No matter that she was not my favorite person, she meant well enough. "I needed to think anyhow. But yes, I worried if I was letting my girlish fancies run away with my common sense."

"Why do you always doubt that I want you?" Mathior looks up at me, his heart in his singular dark eye. The paint on his face is smudged and likely decorating the front of my dress, but I find that I do not care. "Have I not shown you my love?"

I reach down and brush my fingers over his jaw. "Mathior, I'm sorry if I doubted. It's just...I'm so much older than you..."

He growls low in his throat, like an animal, and in the next moment, he lifts me into his arms and carries me as if I weigh nothing. A second later, I'm tossed down onto the bed on my back, and he pushes my skirts up.

I let out a yelp of surprise, pushing them back down. "What are you doing?"

"I'm going to show you just how desirable you are." The look on his face is fierce, as if I've somehow offended him with my worries. "If it means I have to lick that sweet cunt of yours until you come on my face six times, then I will."

"Mathior!" I let out a scandalized gasp even as heat pulses low in my belly.

"You're not old," he tells me as he moves my skirts aside and tugs on my pantaloons. "You are the most beautiful, desirable woman in three kingdoms and I mean to marry you and make you mine. I'm going to keep you in my bed for an entire fortnight until you realize just how perfect you are. And then you're going to tell me that you were wrong."

"I just don't understand why a handsome young king would marry an old spinster with no money," I say, smoothing his hair back from his face as he nuzzles at the inside of my thigh. Riekki have mercy, I should be pushing him away. There's an entire castle full of Yshremi nobility and Cyclopae warriors waiting for our wedding, and here we are in bed. Worse, there's a hole in the door where someone is sure to overhear what we are doing...and yet I find I don't want him to move his head away from that very spot.

"Not old," he says between kisses on my thigh.

"Aventine has a princess," I tell him, fretting. "It would be a good alliance with a port city-state and bring wealth to the kingdoms."

He pushes my thighs farther apart, until I'm sprawled beneath him. "Aventine is a cesspit," he mutters. "Why do you throw other women before me on the brink of our wedding?" His tongue moves over the seam of my pussy, stealing my breath away. "Aventine's princess surely cannot taste nearly as good as the one in my arms right now."

Oh, gods. Mathior says such scandalous things that I feel as if I'm melting into a puddle of heat. "Then...you're marrying me because you want me in your bed?"

He growls again, and I feel it against my core. It sends shivers through my body and I cry out softly. "I'm marrying you because you've been mine from the day you saved my life. I've loved you for sixteen years, Halla. I've fought countless battles and worked my way through the ranks of cyclops warriors to become First Warrior, because I knew that when I was king, I could have you. I've never wanted anything but you." His tongue drags over my folds and then he slides a finger up and down them, teasing them apart. "Do you think I haven't been advised to make political marriages? To quell Yshrem's mutterings in some other way than a wedding?"

Guilt surges through me. "Oh, but—"

"No buts," Mathior says. "I will never give you up. You are mine. Tell me that you'll marry me." He looks up from the cradle of my thighs, his lips hidden by the curls covering my pussy. I can feel his breath there, hot and ticklish, but the look in his gaze is anything but playful.

"I love you," I whisper to him. It seems impossible to be in love this quickly, but he's dazzled me at every moment and keeps right on doing so. "I just want you to do what's best for Cyclopae and Yshrem."

"I am not marrying for Cyclopae," he tells me with a fierce lick that makes me whimper. "I am not marrying for Yshrem." Another lick. "I am marrying you because I want you and I want you to want me."

"I want you."

The look he gives me is ferocious with pleasure. "Then say you'll be my bride and there will be no more of this 'spinster' foolishness."

"I'm yours," I tell him, giving in completely. I've always been his, it seems. I let my head be swayed by the bitter words of an old woman and doubted, but the moment I saw the worry on his face, I knew that he loved me. It's the most amazing feeling. "Oh, Mathior. I'm so afraid to be happy."

"Don't be afraid," he tells me between kisses on my pussy. "I've got you."

"Should..." I gasp, forgetting my thoughts as he flicks his tongue against my clit. "I...oh...wait, Mathior. Shouldn't we get ready for our wedding...oh, gods have mercy." He begins to lick me with light, teasing circles of his tongue against my clit, and it makes me want to roll my hips along with those movements.

"Not yet," he tells me, possessive and sexy all at once. "I want you and I can't wait until the wedding. I'm going to claim my bride now, before she can change her mind again." A thick finger presses against the entrance to my core, then begins to tease at the entrance, and I feel hollow and achy and so wild that I writhe in the bed, lifting my hips up against his vexing mouth. "Right now."

"But your customs..."

He presses his mouth against me, like a hot brand. "Damn the customs. Let them snicker at how their king couldn't wait to bed his bride. It doesn't matter. They will laugh and tease me, but in the end, I will have you. What do I care of what they think?"

I gasp, clutching at his head as he swipes his tongue over my folds. It feels so good and yet... "No."

He lifts his head at that. "What?"

"You said yourself that the customs matter. That your people are proud of who they are. Why would we not honor all of them? We can wait a few hours." I lightly run my fingers over his face, touching his scar, the paint that covers it, everything. "I would have you honored."

Mathior thinks for a moment. He nips at the inside of my thigh, and it's clear he does not want to leave just yet. "Halla..."

I add primly, "I would also have you remember that you stripped me naked before your entire court."

Mathior buries his head between my thighs and laughs, shoulders shaking. "So I did. Very well. We shall complete the wedding as it should be done, and let no one say that my will is not as steel." He gives my pussy one last kiss, sighs heavily, and then gets off the bed. "Shall we go and get married, then?"

When he extends his hand to me, I clasp it and stand, then straighten my clothing. There is red paint all over my skirts and hands, and the symbols on his body are smeared. "I think we should probably clean up first."

"More delays," he mutters, and gives a shake of his head. "Then I need one more kiss before I can let you go." He pulls me close and kisses me until I'm breathless, and then finally releases me and studies my face, then wipes a smear of red off of it. "I see now why warriors cover themselves with paint before a wedding—it's so everyone knows the bride is untouched by his hands."

I blush at that.

He caresses my cheek. "Bathe fast. I know I shall."

"I will," I promise him. And I mean it. My doubts are gone and I want nothing more than to marry this man and see what life will hold for us. I grab his hand as he turns away and press a kiss to his knuckles. "I'm sorry if I scared you."

"If I touch you again, we will not be leaving this room," he warns, but doesn't pull his hand from my grip.

I chuckle and let my tongue flick over his skin before I release him.

13

HALLA

*T*he wedding ceremony is a blur.

I should be focusing on the ritual of it all, but the only thing I can think of is Mathior. I scarcely see the hundreds of people lining the great hall—Yshremi and Cyclopae both. I pay no attention to the priests and the prayers they send up on our behalf. The vows, the songs sung over us, even my coronation—none of it matters.

I can think of nothing more than getting back to my rooms with my new husband and finishing what we started.

Mathior's hand touches mine frequently throughout the wedding, caressing my fingers, and when he lifts my hand to his mouth to kiss and tongues my knuckles instead, I know he's thinking about the same thing. It makes me blush and the room fills with cheers.

I am every dazzled bride on her wedding day, and I am also now queen of Yshrem and Cyclopae and Adassia. For some reason, that feels less important than being Mathior's wife, though. His smiles are everything, and I clutch at his hand as we sit on our thrones in front of the crowd and let ambassador after ambassador offer their well-wishes, their greetings, and their gifts. Horses and fine dishes are given to us, gold and jewels and spices from faraway lands. There's a flute of pure crystal from Citadel, fine silks and rich offerings of grain from Glistentide, and a pair of finely forged steel-swords from Aventine, which makes Mathior glance over at me.

Those will be promptly stored away somewhere safe, I decide. I also tell myself I can't be jealous since it was my idea.

There is a royal feast, full of pastries and cooked dishes from Yshrem and Cyclopae alike. I eat a bite of everything as is polite, but I taste nothing. I'm unable to concentrate because Mathior sits at my side and reaches for my hand from time to time. Are all brides like this on their wedding day, I wonder? Because I cannot think of anything except what is to come...and how eager I am for it. I think about the book with the pictures far more than is seemly, and I think about Mathior and his mouth, and last night.

"Come," a delicious voice says in my ear and I shiver. For a moment, I think it's a command, but when I look up, Mathior is extending his hand to me. "It's time."

Dazed, I rise to my feet, and as I do, the room erupts into cheers. I look at the sea of faces—Yshremi and Cyclopae alike—and see nothing but gladness. If there are rebellious dissenters who think I am betraying my country, they are not here. Perhaps they are very few, and in time, there will not be many at all.

It doesn't matter. I've chosen my path and I am happy with it. No, more than happy—I am giddy with delight. I squeeze Mathior's hand as I move to his side, and we exit from the great hall with as much dignity as possible.

Yshrem's halls seem endless as we walk toward our private chambers. My heart trips in my breast as I realize we're not going to my rooms, but to his. Of course we are. My bed is lovely, but it is only built for one. Now I am Mathior's bride and I will never sleep alone again.

We sweep down the longest hallway that leads to a familiar wing of the castle, and I feel a little uneasy. This is the wing that housed my father's chambers. I clutch at Mathior's arm a little tighter, because I don't know if I can go into Father's rooms with my Cyclopae husband. Somehow that seems wrong. But we turn down a separate corridor and head toward a different room instead. I let out a sigh of relief when I see that Mathior has claimed the ambassador's quarters as his own.

He glances down at me and his expression is full of understanding. "No matter how I felt about your father, it didn't seem right to take his rooms. I figure when the baby arrives, we can establish them as a nursery."

"Baby?" I echo.

"Not yet, but hopefully soon." Mathior gives me a confident look.

Unease shivers through me. "I might be too old—"

"Nonsense. You are thirty-three, not eighty-three." He notices people watching us and leans closer so our words can be private. "I am told my mother was one year older than you when my father met and married her."

Oh.

He squeezes my hand. "And if there is no baby, well...it will be a good chamber for my horse."

I stare up at him, aghast, and then realize he's joking. A horrified laugh erupts from me, and then I'm snort-giggling as we enter our rooms. There are servants waiting here, and they bow and make their way out as we enter. Mathior is silent, but a smile curves his mouth. The servants grin as they hurry away, and I just feel...happy. Weirdly happy and content.

Mathior turns and watches as the last of the servants trail out of the room. He shuts the door behind them and then slides the bar across to ensure we will be alone. Once that is done, he turns to look at me. "My queen."

He makes it sound like a secret whispered between lovers, and I tremble. "My king."

"Yours alone." He unclasps his fur cloak and tosses it aside, revealing a chest covered with bright red symbols. This time, the paint is dry and the markings unmarred. I can't help but stare, because the painted lines and curves emphasize the warm color of his skin and the hard bulge of his muscles. I'm getting flustered and aroused just looking at him.

And I can't stop staring.

My new husband stalks to my side, searching my face. He cups my chin. "Still all right, or do you need to rest?"

"I'm fine." I truly am. Overwhelmed, yes, but ready for this. In a way, the last two shocking ceremonies have prepared me for this night. Instead of being nervous and afraid of what it will bring, I'm full of anticipation for my husband's touch. I lean in against him and press my hand over the symbol of the axe across his broad chest. "This is for Aron of the Cleaver?" I guess, because we were married in the Hour of Storms, the time that is sacred to the god of battle.

"Aye. We cyclops pray to him more than any other."

I gaze up at him and at the scar over his eye. "I see that."

"Do you regret that you have married a man with only one eye?" He traces his finger down the scarred line on his face. "I know you remember me with two."

"It was...startling to see, but I don't regret it, no." I follow the path his finger took and trace the scar myself. "You are proud of your people. I understand this. I wouldn't ask you to change."

"That is a good thing, as I can't put my eye back," he teases.

"You know what I mean," I tell him, pinching his chin between my fingers and giving his head a little shake. "If you are proud of it, I am too. You look different, but everything about you is different now. It doesn't make it unpleasant."

"Shall I wear my eyepatch for you?"

"If you like." He didn't wear it during the wedding, and while I was shocked at first, I enjoy seeing his face without anything to hide it. "But I think you are handsome either way."

He grins and snags my hand, then presses a kiss to my palm. "I should wash this paint off. Would you like to help?"

My pulse flutters at the thought. I can feel myself growing shy... but at the same time, I do want to touch him. "I think I would."

Mathior slides a hand down my back and then cups my ass briefly before releasing me. "Then come and let us get started."

I let him lead me over to the wash-basin and towels that have been left behind by the servants. Before I can ask if he wants me to undress him, Mathior shucks his boots and strips off his leggings. Utterly silent—and more than a little shocked—I watch as he gets completely naked within a matter of moments, and then I am staring at his bare backside. I'm not surprised to see that he's less tanned in the places that do not see sunlight, but I am a little startled at how much I'm affected by the sight of his tight backside.

I saw this the other day, of course, when we were in the great hall. But we were not alone, then, and I did not have the leisure to touch. And I want to touch him very much. I move forward and slide a hand down his bare back.

He groans and stiffens as I caress him. I half-expect Mathior to tell me to stop or to push my hand away because I'm distracting him. Instead, he dunks the towel into the basin and then holds the dripping thing out to me.

Oh.

I take it and tentatively slide the towel over one brawny arm. Water droplets, now pink from the running paint, sluice down his skin and I'm fascinated at the sight of them. I let the towel trail over his bicep, slowly moving it up one shoulder and then across his back. His long hair is getting in the way, so I wrap it around my hand and lift it, then glide the towel further.

Mathior groans. "I'm not sure if this is a bath or a tease."

"Can it be both?"

"Obviously." He casts a grin over his shoulder at me and he's the most beautiful man I've ever seen.

I swipe the towel over his shoulders one more time and then release his hair, watching it spill down his damp skin with a dreamy sigh. Mathior turns and holds out his other arm, and I run the cloth over it, too. My cheeks pink when I realize he's not looking at what I'm doing, but at me instead. I feel beautiful and sexy and truly seen. I move the towel over his muscles, fascinated by him. I've seen him shirtless plenty of times before—in fact, I don't think I've ever seen him with a shirt on—but to be able to touch him like this changes everything.

He turns slightly and then he's facing me, and as I slide the wet towel forward over his chest and on the axe symbol, I glance down. I was too shy to look at him in the great hall at the revealing ceremony, not with everyone calling out at us. But now I can look my fill.

His cock is...enormous. It's hard and erect with need, a gleaming droplet poised on the tip. His skin is flushed a darker color here, and a faint, dark trail on his belly leads down to black curls that frame his erection and the sac underneath. A large vein traces down his length, and I itch to touch it and explore it with my mouth. Just the thought makes me feel flushed and breathless, and I glance up at my new husband to see if he feels the same.

"Touch me," he demands, voice low and husky. A shiver of excitement moves through me and I don't protest when he snags the towel out of my hand and tosses it aside. All I care about is touching him, learning his body.

I let my fingertips graze over the head of his cock, and I'm surprised at how scorchingly hot his skin is...and how soft. It feels like silk over iron as I drift my way down his length with small touches, caressing and exploring. Mathior holds himself very still as I caress his length. It's like he doesn't want to interrupt or distract me. I encircle his girth with my fingers and they don't touch. I'm surprised at how thick he is. I knew he was long, but the cock I'm touching seems very different from the one I saw in the great hall two days ago at the revealing. "You're much larger today."

The breath huffs out of him in a laugh. "The entire world is not staring at my cock to judge it. I only need to impress you." The backs of his fingers graze my cheek. "What do you think?"

"I like it," I tell him softly. "But I am not entirely certain that the two of us will fit together. Are cyclops warriors built differently than Yshremi men?"

"They kept you far too sheltered at that temple," Mathior says, amused. He steps forward, thrusting his length further into my grip, and then he grabs me by the ornate braid hanging down my back and tilts my head until I'm gazing up at him. "In a way, I'm glad. It means you're completely mine."

"Yours and only yours," I whisper back, and he kisses me.

Our hungry mouths meet and his tongue teases mine, the kisses growing deeper and more frantic the longer we touch. I can't help but stroke the thick length of him with my hand, and when he groans into my mouth, it makes me bolder and I want to do it again. I rub his cock once more, eager to pleasure him.

He pulls away from my lips at the same time he removes my hand, and I let out a whimper of protest. "I want you undressed," Mathior tells me, and tugs at the laces of my gown. The dress I wore for my wedding was a mixture of my world and his. My gown was made of the same pale lavender that symbolizes Yshrem, with laces up each side to hug my figure. The long bell sleeves and skirt are trimmed with white fur that matches Mathior's cloak, as does the wide fur collar that skims my shoulders and leaves them bare. It's a beautiful gown, I note absently, and now we've ruined it with red paint splashes and water. I don't care. I'm allowed to touch my husband—my king.

There will be other dresses.

He grips the laces and I hold my breath, waiting for him to rip them away. He doesn't, though; he gently tugs them free of their knots and then lets the cord slide to the ground. One side, then the other, and then my dress hangs off of my body like a sack. He takes the material and pulls it over my head, and then I'm in nothing but a corset and pantaloons, just like I was in the great hall.

This is different, though, just like he said. Everything is different.

My new husband stares at my body so intently that I prickle all over. The red paint has left streaks down his chest and arms, but I don't care. I'm trembling with the need for him to touch me and smear that paint all over my body, skin to skin. Slowly, he tugs at the bow binding the lacings of my corset together and pulls it free. The material falls open, gaping, and he works the ties down, tugging them free until the entire thing falls off of my body and pools at my feet. I'm holding my breath as he stares at me, and I want desperately for him to touch me. I need him, my pulse thrumming between my thighs like my heart is there. When he doesn't move to touch me, I get impatient and slide my pantaloons down my legs with a shimmy until I'm naked before him, like he is to me.

"Beautiful," he tells me. With one hand, he reaches out and runs his knuckles over the tip of one aching breast.

I gasp at that small touch, wanting so much more and yet shocked at how exposed it makes me feel.

He puts a hand to my waist and pulls me against him, and then his cock is pressing up against my belly like a branding iron, hot and insistent. He captures my mouth in another scorching kiss, and as he does, his hand moves to my breast. His thumb rubs over the nipple, back and forth, teasing it into an aching point as his tongue flicks against mine. Desire, hot and giddy, rushes through me and I cling to him.

"I'm taking you to the bed," he murmurs between kisses, and I don't argue. I want that. I want him in every possible way. So I loop my arms around his neck as he hauls me against him and carries me across the chamber. I feel the fur of his blankets against my backside a moment before he gently sets me down, and then I'm tumbling backward into the bed with his weight on top of me.

There's no time to be nervous, not with his skin pressed against mine, chest to chest, our arms twined around each other. I love the feel of him against my body, and when he slides a thigh between mine, I eagerly lift one leg and twine it around his hip. He settles in against me, and I can feel his cock resting against my pussy. It feels like he was meant to be there, and I'm in love with how right it feels. How right he feels.

He nips at my mouth, taking soft, playful kisses as he gazes down at me. "My beautiful wife. My Halla. I've waited for this day forever."

His loving words make me shy and I give him a smile, moving my hands over him. His hair is sliding over one shoulder onto my body and I want to cover myself in its silky feel. "I'm glad it's finally here." The last three days have seemed endless.

Mathior kisses me again, his hand going back to my breast and teasing my nipple. "Are you nervous?"

It's hard to concentrate when he's touching me like this. Nervous? Never. I trust him. I shake my head, utterly confident in my husband.

"This is my first time," he confesses, fascinated by my breasts. He slides a bit lower, kissing down my neck and shoulder, and then making his way down to my breasts. His hand goes to my belly and he nips at the slope of one rounded globe.

My eyes widen in surprise at his words. I'm distracted by his teasing mouth, so perhaps I haven't heard correctly. "You've never...?"

He shakes his head. "Of course not. I waited for you."

I am speechless. Overwhelmed by his sweet confession, I pull him back up to me and kiss him. "I love you," I tell him for what feels like the hundredth time today. How could I not trust this man? I feel like such a fool. A giddy, lucky fool, but a fool nevertheless.

Mathior chuckles against my mouth and kisses me back. "I told you it has always been you, lovely Halla, and I meant it." He bites my lower lip gently, and I moan against him. "Always you."

"Love you," I whisper again. Was ever any princess as lucky as me?

His hips fit against mine once more, and when he guides my legs around his waist, I eagerly encircle him, ready for what comes next. Mathior kisses me again, and as he does, I feel him slide a hand between our bodies. In the next moment, something hard presses against my core—his cock. Before I have time to be nervous, his hips surge forward and then he's pushing into me.

The breath chokes out of me in a gasp. I thought I was ready, but this feels tight and uncomfortable, like I'd always been told sex would be. I thought it would be different with Mathior, and I let out a little whimper of distress at this realization.

"It'll only hurt the first time," he says, soothing me with kisses. "I'm sorry, love."

I hold on to him as he remains completely still over me, nuzzling my face and kissing my unhappiness away. One moment bleeds into the next, and when he shifts his weight, his hips rocking against mine, I'm surprised to feel that it's not as uncomfortable as it was just a moment ago, and that I love the feel of him pinning me down. I brush my lips against his and when he flexes again, this time I flex with him.

Mathior groans, and his kisses become more urgent. He rocks into me again, and there's a sharp bite of discomfort that's quickly gone, and then there's nothing but the intense feeling of him deep inside me, filling me completely. I've never felt anything quite like it and I can't catch my breath. It's like he's piercing me all the way to my heart.

And then he moves, and everything changes again. With one slow stroke, pleasure ripples up, and I moan, closing my eyes.

"That's it," he murmurs, his hand stroking down the side of my neck, my shoulder, even as he covers my face with urgent kisses. He pushes deep into me again, and then begins a slow, delicious rhythm that teases every doubt out of my mind. "Hold on to me, love."

I twine my arms around his neck, clinging to him even as he pumps into my body. Yesterday's "tasting" was nothing but wonderful sensations, and a coil of need that built slowly in my belly until I went over the edge. I feel that same coil starting again, and a moan escapes me. My husband whispers my name and begins to move faster, and as he does, the pleasure grows.

I raise my hips to meet his, and it only adds to the friction between us. Each stroke becomes more forceful, deeper, stronger, and far more pleasurable. The blankets are bunching up underneath my back with the force of his thrusts, but I don't want to stop. I want him to keep going and going. The spiral low in my belly grows, but then he stops, pressing his forehead to mine.

"Oh, no," I whimper frantically, my hands plucking at him. "Keep going. I'm so close."

"You are?" He lifts his head and then groans at the expression on my face, taking my mouth in a fierce kiss. His hand cups my breast, kneading it even as he thrusts, and I moan again. It's good, but I'm not there yet.

"Faster," I urge him. "More."

With a low, feral growl, he does just that. He's thrusting so hard into me that our bodies have skimmed over the surface of the bed and my shoulder is anchored next to the wooden headboard. I press against it, trying to brace myself even as I surge my hips up against his. I need more. More. More. It's so good, but I'm still not quite there.

"Please," I whisper, the urgent feeling washing over me. I bite down on my lip and arch up against him. "Mathior!"

He rocks into me hard, and when I make a noise of frustration, his hand slips between us. "Come for me," he demands, and a second later, I feel his thumb slide over my clit. "Need you to come first, Halla."

The next time he thrusts, it moves his thumb against my clit, rubbing, and that's all I need. With a wild cry, I lock one arm around his neck and bury my face against it, biting and kissing and licking as I quake in a fierce climax. He pumps into me again, and I'm barely aware of the breath hissing from his throat as his body stiffens over mine. He keeps rubbing my clit, though, his hand jerking and twitching against my sensitive spots as he shudders over me.

Eventually, the climax slides away and I moan when he rubs his thumb against my clit again. I realize absently that he's collapsed on top of me, his weight pressing me down into the bed. I like the feel of it, of his sweaty skin against mine, our bodies joined. I do feel slippery, though, especially between my thighs where our juices have mingled.

Mathior lifts his head, his long hair spilling over both of us. He gives me a dazed kiss. "Halla. That was...better than I anticipated. And I have anticipated a lot in the last sixteen years."

I chuckle, because I know how he feels. I am without words...just happy. Blissfully, wonderfully happy.

And when he leans in to kiss me again, I wonder how long it'll be before we can do that again.

EPILOGUE

MATHIOR

"*H*e has your eyes," I tell Halla, watching with fascination as my son grips my finger with a tiny hand. "And my sword-arm, I think."

"Better your sword-arm than mine," my lovely wife says. She doesn't lift her head from the pillow but gives me a blissfully happy look. "Are you glad it's a son?"

I gaze down at the baby in my arms. Am I? A son is fine, but I would be happy with a daughter that looked like her mother, too. That will be next, I decide. Halla thinks she is old, but we still have many good years between us, and she's as eager for bedplay as I am. Perhaps more so. My innocent, sheltered wife loves to torture me with her mouth in all the best ways. Just thinking about it makes my cock harden, and I push such thoughts aside. It will be weeks or months before Halla is ready to join me in bed again, and I will wait.

I will always wait for her.

"I am glad our child is happy and healthy," I tell her, tucking our son into the crook of my arm and moving closer to the bed so I can kiss her brow. She's tired and disheveled after the birth but smiling. "I want nothing more than that."

Halla's sleepy chuckle is beautiful to hear.

"You feel well enough?" I rock the baby in my arms and watch her closely. I am very aware of the fact that her mother died in childbirth. It is a worry that has consumed me for weeks on end. But Halla has been inspected by every healer and clerist I can find and determined to be very healthy after the birth of our child a few short hours ago.

She waves a hand at me and yawns. "Merely sleepy. Quit worrying. You try having a baby and see how energetic you are."

"I shall have the next one," I promise her, and I'm delighted when she giggles. I live for her laughter. "Have you decided on a name, then?"

"Alistair," my lovely wife tells me with an adoring smile.

My heart clenches and I'm filled with a rush of love. I look down at the boy in my arms, with his small, perfect face. He's reddish from the birth and wrinkly, but to me he's as wondrous as his mother. She knows how much I loved my father, even if we didn't agree on many things. "Alistair, then," I say softly.

She reaches a hand out to me and squeezes mine. "Now, we should go and show our people our son."

"I will," I tell her, and lean over the bed to give her another kiss first. "Have I told you that I love you, my beautiful Queen Halla?"

"Only twice today," she tells me with a yawn. "You're slipping."

"I love you," I say fervently, and I mean it. My hunger for my Halla hasn't lessened in the slightest over the last year of our marriage. If anything, it's only grown deeper, like my love for her. "You are everything to me."

"I love you, too," my wife says, and offers her palm for a kiss. I take it and press my mouth against it. A second later, I'm surprised when she starts to get out of bed.

"What are you doing?"

"We're going to present our son, are we not?" She wraps the furs around her body, grimacing at the aches she must feel. "Give me the baby and you can carry us both out onto the balcony."

She wants to go with me? I laugh, but I'm not surprised. My wife is as fierce as any cyclops warrior in her way, and she always gets what she wants. I carefully transfer the baby—Alistair—to her arms—and then pick her up in mine. I grunt a little at that. "It feels like you've still got a baby in you."

Halla snorts and gives me a wry look. "Not what you want to tell your wife after she's just had your child."

"My wife knows she's beautiful beyond words."

She looks up at my face and smiles. "She does."

And I take my wife and child out onto the balcony of Castle Yshrem and show the people—Cyclopae and Yshremi and Adassian alike—my family.

AUTHOR'S NOTE

You're invited to the wedding of the century...times four!

When the Club ladies heard about the upcoming royal wedding, we immediately knew we wanted to do our own spin on it. We're romantics at heart, and a royal wedding is pretty much the pinnacle of happy ever after. Each story's going to be different (despite the fun matching covers) with one overarching theme – a king and his bride. I'm so excited for everyone to read all four stories!

Also, a total shout out to Kati Wilde for her magnificent cover art. I love every aspect of it, right down to the wedding invitation look. You guys know (if you follow me on Facebook) that Kati does all my covers, and I love each one more and more. I feel truly blessed that I get to work with her. Kati, a million thank yous once again for being a friend and collaborator! Let's be honest, though – the Ruby end of the collaboration is usually "He looks hot and he's blue! What can you do with that?" and Kati always somehow makes it magic.

As for this particular story...every author out there has a few story ideas saved up on her hard drive that she's dying to get to but doesn't have the time. This particular one was on my hard drive as 'The Cyclops Bride' for at least the last two or three years. I'd pick it up, read my outline and get ready to write...and then something else would land on my plate and on a back-burner it'd go. So when we talked royal weddings, I immediately pulled this one out of the pile. I'm so thrilled to get the chance to write Mathior and Halla FINALLY. I've never written a 'cougar' story and damn, that was fun. I'll have to do that again. ;)

On the 9th of May, **Kati Wilde**'s *The King's Horrible Bride* will be releasing! May 10th, **Alexa Riley**'s *The King's Innocent Bride* and on May 11th, **Ella Goode**'s *The King's Reluctant Bride* hits. These will ALL be in Kindle Unlimited, so you can borrow all of them to your heart's content. It'll be like prepping for the big day.

Enjoy! <3

Ruby

PS – Since we're only human and sometimes publishing doesn't go the way it should with glitches and all, the dates are MOSTLY PRETTY MUCH FINGERS CROSSED in stone but if there's a burp, one might be late in going up. Just keep watching or sign up on Facebook to follow The Club and we'll let you know when each one hits!

RUBY DIXON READING LIST

FIREBLOOD DRAGONS

Fire in His Blood
Fire in His Kiss
Fire in His Embrace
Fire in His Fury

ICE PLANET BARBARIANS

Ice Planet Barbarians
Barbarian Alien
Barbarian Lover
Barbarian Mine
Ice Planet Holiday (novella)
Barbarian's Prize
Barbarian's Mate
Having the Barbarian's Baby (short story)
Ice Ice Babies (short story)
Barbarian's Touch

Calm(short story)
Barbarian's Taming
Aftershocks (short story)
Barbarian's Heart
Barbarian's Hope
Barbarian's Choice
Barbarian's Redemption
Barbarian's Lady
Barbarian's Rescue
Barbarian's Tease
The Barbarian Before Christmas (novella)
Barbarian's Beloved

CORSAIRS
THE CORSAIR'S CAPTIVE
IN THE CORSAIR'S BED
ENTICED BY THE CORSAIR

STAND ALONE

PRISON PLANET BARBARIAN
THE ALIEN'S MAIL-ORDER BRIDE
BEAUTY IN AUTUMN

BEDLAM BUTCHERS
Bedlam Butchers, Volumes 1-3: Off Limits, Packing Double,
Double Trouble
Bedlam Butchers, Volumes 4-6: Double Down, Double or
Nothing, Slow Ride
Double Dare You

BEAR BITES
Shift Out of Luck

Get Your Shift Together
Shift Just Got Real
Does A Bear Shift in the Woods
SHIFT: Five Complete Novellas

WANT MORE?

For more information about upcoming books in the Ice Planet Barbarians, Fireblood Dragons, or any other books by Ruby Dixon, 'like' me on Facebook or subscribe to my new release newsletter. If you want to chat about the books, why not also check out the Blue Barbarian Babes fan group?

Thanks for reading!

<3 Ruby